Perelman's Refusal: A Novel

Perelman's Refusal: A Novel

Philippe Zaouati

Translated by Rachel Zerner

AMERICAN MATHEMATICAL SOCIETY

Providence, Rhode Island

2020 *Mathematics Subject Classification.* Primary 01A70.

For additional information and updates on this book, visit
www.ams.org/bookpages/mbk-137

This work was originally published in French by PIPPA Editions under the title
Les Refus de Grigori Perelman ©2017. The present translation was created under
license for the American Mathematical Society and it is published by permission.

The quote on page vii by Hermann Hesse, *Steppenwolf,* was translated by Basil
Creighton (Updated by Joseph Mileck), ©1963 by Holt, Rinehart and Winston,
Inc.

Library of Congress Cataloging-in-Publication Data
Names: Zaouati, Philippe, author. | Zerner, Rachel, translator.
Title: Perelman's Refusal : A Novel / Philippe Zaouati ; translated by: Rachel Zerner.
Other titles: Les Refus de Grigori Perelman. English.
Description: Providence, Rhode Island : American Mathematical Society, [2021] | "This work
    was originally published in French by PIPPA Editions under the title *Les Refus de Grigori
    Perelman* ©2017."
Identifiers: LCCN 2020050084 | ISBN 9781470463045 (paperback) | ISBN 9781470464905 (ebook)
Subjects: LCSH: Perelman, Grigori, 1966—Fiction. | Mathematicians–Russia (Federation)–
    Fiction. | AMS: History and biography–History of mathematics and mathematicians–Biogra-
    phies, obituaries, personalia, bibliographies.
Classification: LCC PQ2726.A586 R4413 2021 | DDC 843/.92–dc23
LC record available at https://lccn.loc.gov/2020050084

For Sacha

"The tragedy of human existence is having to one day to renounce being in the light." Hubert Reeves, *Intimes Convictions*.

"For he was not a sociable man. Indeed, he was unsociable to a degree I had never before experienced in anybody." Hermann Hesse, *Steppenwolf*.

Contents

June 10, 2006

A moment of triumph, however fleeting, is certainly worth a bit of effort, and even sacrifice. When John Ball accepted the mission his colleagues entrusted him with, he had immediately perceived its challenges. Virtually impossible, he had thought. But were he to pull it off, what a coup it would be!

In the plane that would soon deposit him at the international airport in Saint Petersburg, he felt thoroughly determined and keyed up. After all, he was a secret agent after a fashion, a James Bond, on her Majesty's secret service you might say, ready for feats of derring do… He was, however, a James Bond who had neither electronic gadgets nor a fully loaded Aston Martin. Sir John Ball would have no need for them. His were subtler weapons. He would have to rely on intelligence and persuasion.

Throughout the long hours of flight time connecting London with the former capital of the Tsars, he had reviewed various bulging files and considered the facts of the matter, working on an approach. Once again, John Ball combed over the slightest details of the life and psychology of the individual he had come to meet on his home turf, to make him see reason. And reason, in John Ball's world, held a place most people could hardly imagine.

Reason was not, for him, a relative notion. Nor was it a topic to be debated by students in Philosophy 101. No indeed, reason was a formidable process. It was this implacable capacity for refutation and demonstration that he and his colleagues—a few thousand beings all told—pushed to the threshold of the sublime by force of mind. For John Ball belonged to a community that could fairly be described as arcane, or even occult. It wasn't that its members claimed to be protecting any kind of secret. It wasn't that they were hiding a priceless relic or immeasurable treasure. Nothing like that. It was just that the power and complexity of the investigations they were involved in set them apart from their fellow human beings.

John Ball was a mathematician, an eminent one. His was one of a handful of minds capable of discussing how movement takes place in worlds that don't exist. One able to calculate distances in the fourth or even fifth dimensions. His was a genius unshackled by the limited reality our five senses perceive.

And it was as a mathematician that he would have to navigate the trial facing him today. The battle he was about to fight would have no swordplay, and he would have to win over his "adversary" entirely on the strength of whatever arguments his intelligence and skill could muster. Meaning he would be fighting with words. Nothing but words …

He had two days.

His briefcase was black, its leather sides scuffed and sagging. It looked like the bags once carried by country doctors. In it, John Ball had slipped his reading glasses, the day's papers, a novel in French and a fat folder with elastic bands. This contained a hodgepodge of pages that included photocopies from academic math journals, newspaper clippings, website printouts and a handful of pictures. Taken all together, it was a file bristling with items but without any obvious logic. Leafing quickly through the longer documents, he would here and there highlight a passage, jumping from one text to another. Suddenly his attention fixed on an almost empty sheet of paper. A single sentence in bold type ran across the top of the page, its isolation lending it a solemn quality, like a biblical quote: "A topological sphere is the only compact three-dimensional space without boundaries."[1] Turning it over, he found a barely legible handwritten note scrawled across the right corner. Presumably, it had been written by Ball's assistant, who had put together the file to help his boss prepare for the trip. It read: "Must read. Poincaré's Conjecture for dummies. My six-year old son could understand it." There followed some thirty lines of printed text, entirely in italics. It seemed to be an extract from the blog of some amateur mathematician who had feebly attempted to explain one of the 20th century's most famous mathematical mysteries.

The media focus on the impenetrable quality of the Poincaré Conjecture. In its broad lines, however, it is quite possible to explain the issue.

Start with a manifold of dimension 2. Imagine a sort of potato in space. Make it as knobby as you like, with lumps and dimples—think of the title characters in the "Barbapapa" cartoon, but without any actual holes. Here, we are interested in the skin of our potato, its surface. Imagine it malleable, made of Play-Doh or something similar. We can then stretch it until it becomes a smooth, perfectly round ball. In a word,

---

[1] The traditional formulation of the Poincaré Conjecture in English reads: "Is every simply connected 3-manifold topologically equivalent to the 3-sphere?"

a sphere. Such is the Poincaré Conjecture for dimension 2. In mathematics, surfaces are dimension 2. OK, are you with me? Now, the question is, does this still hold in dimension 3? This is what people have been trying to prove since Poincaré first published his conjecture in 1904. Mathematicians are certain that Poincaré was correct, but no one had succeeded in proving it... Until Grigori Perelman.

You have to imagine a volume—a dimension 3 object—surrounded by 4-dimensional space. What is dimension 4 space, you ask? One might answer that this is "time-space" but that would hardly make things any clearer. The fact remains that in mathematics, it exists. A space may have any number of dimensions. So, let us imagine a "volume" in 4-dimensional space. Make it reasonably lumpy and, this is important, free of holes. We can therefore distend it until it becomes a dimension-3 sphere. But, what is a dimension-3 sphere? Perhaps this is exactly the space we operate in...

And there you have a rough approximation of the Conjecture submitted by the great mathematician Henri Poincaré. With considerable prescience, he had noted that: "the answer would take us too far afield."

John Ball was no expert in topology. Mathematicians, like everyone else, have their areas of expertise. There are specialties, like in medicine. A cardiac surgeon would be stymied faced with a cataract operation, and mathematicians are knowledgeable only within the circumscribed perimeter of their research. It is said that Poincaré was one of the last great generalists. He could move from a problem in geometry to equations in astronomy or fluid dynamics. At ease discussing the shape of the universe, he happily combined philosophy and math. Those were different times. A world when the sum of human knowledge remained approachable for a single, brilliant mind. John Ball had fantasized about it. Encyclopedic knowledge… it must have been so exciting. Today, genius itself is condemned to restrict its dancing to the head of a pin.

John Ball was no topologist, but he was familiar with the Poincaré conjecture, naturally. He had learned as a youth that a teacup with a handle and a donut with a hole are exactly the same thing, topologically speaking. With a modicum of imagination one can morph the former into the latter, and vice-versa. Thus, do the trivial specificities of reality yield to the irrefutable superiority of the concept. And, for an Englishman, any concept that starts with a teacup is by definition a comforting one.

John Ball also knew full well what a connected space, finite in size and lacking any boundary, is. How many times had he demonstrated a 3-manifold to first-year students using an orange and a needle and thread? Drive the needle into the orange anywhere, wrap the thread around back to the needle and pull slowly. Eventually, the loop of thread closes until it is tight around the needle—reduced to a single point. Next, you try it with a teacup, or a donut, making sure that the thread passes through the hole in the object on its way back to the needle. This time, when you pull the string it remains stuck around the donut. No matter how hard you try, you cannot turn your donut into an orange. "Where two-dimensional surfaces are concerned, at any rate, topology is singularly food-focused," thought the mathematician to himself, smiling.

The flight attendant offered him a drink. Whisky, he accepted gratefully. With ice.

As though to convince himself of its veracity, he read the sentence from the front of the page over again. "A topological sphere is the only compact three-dimensional space without boundaries." Such is the formulation of the Poincaré Conjecture. It certainly seemed reasonable. Poincaré wasn't likely to have been wrong. Why shouldn't something that was true for a two-dimensional surface be true in dimension three as well?

The entire towering edifice of mathematics required that the Conjecture be true. What's more, it was hardly a topic of doubt. For more than a century, the best minds in all mathematics had obstinately battled to arrive at the proof of a property they all considered a given.

Except none of them had made it ...

Until Grigori Perelman.

The taxi swung into a side street perpendicular to Nevsky Prospekt, along the Moyka River. The driver came a halt before the entrance of the hotel whose name John Ball had given. The Hotel Kempinski was a posh aristocratic residence from the mid-nineteenth century that had recently undergone extensive renovations. Three balconies adorned the building's facade, one to each side on the first story, and one at the center of the third. Each was richly decked with colorful flowers. The portico entrance faced one of the fifteen bridges that span the river, almost all of which play some role or other in Russian history or literature. This one was known as the Green bridge, for reasons that were obvious.

John Ball clambered hurriedly out of the taxi, leaving the driver a generous tip. He did not take the time to admire the hotel's architecture. He didn't even glance at the iron arch of the bridge or the riverside dock.

If truth be told, John Ball was not thinking about mathematics, nor the strange personality of Grigori Perelman. He wasn't even contemplating the uncomfortable position of the International Mathematical Union, of which he had been president for the last three years. He was much more concerned with his watch, and proceeded to check it every three minutes. He quickly dropped his minimal baggage at the hotel's reception desk with instructions that it be taken to his room. In fact, his sole preoccupation, his overwhelming concern was this: would he arrive in time to watch the start of England v. Paraguay? This was to be the Roses' first match of the football World Cup, soccer for barbarians. His seatmate on the plane had been an especially loquacious Russian businessman. While John Ball hadn't fully understood the exact nature of the man's business, the latter had provided the address of a bar less than half a mile from the hotel. Apparently, most games were streamed on big screen TVs there. A true sports bar, and a favorite hangout among fans of the Zenith, the local soccer team. He decided to walk. It was exactly five-ten p.m. when he walked into the bar, two hours more than in Frankfurt, where the match was being played.

The Russian businessman had not steered him wrong. The ceiling above the bar counter was festooned with Zenith's turquoise pennants, bearing a five-pointed yellow star and an inscription evoking the club's creation in 1925. The first half had just begun. He sat down at a small wooden table, its surface pocked with cigarette burns and stained with alcohol. He ordered a Baltika. When travelling, wherever he might be in the world, he had adopted the habit of drinking only local beer. In fact, he could go on for hours about the relative merits of Chilean Escudo vs Spain's San Miguel. Or Polish Zywiek, for that matter. A few British fans, already sozzled, were agitating in front of the screen. Probably expat salesmen and bankers. A young redhead with round cheeks was sitting at the bar, proudly draped in the Union Jack. John turned to the screen and realized that Britain was already winning, 1-0. He had missed what was to be the game's only goal. The rest was underwhelming. The redhead fell asleep, her head in the lap of a big blond fellow who regularly erupted into insults against the UK players. "Numbskulls!" "Lazy bastards!" Groups of young Russians wandered in and out, seemingly without reason. John Ball wondered if things were more intense around Covent Garden.

He left the bar right after the whistle blew on the match. He was surprised to find himself savoring his team's victory. The weather was fine. Tourists had poured in from all over Europe to enjoy the "white nights", those miraculous days around the summer solstice when the sun gives way to a sort of gentle twilight only around midnight. The Neva unfurls like a dark blue ribbon around the Neoclassical and Baroque palaces, their façades lit up by powerful projectors reflected in its slow waters. The terrace seating of the restaurants was hopping. Drifting up from cafés and festival bandstands was every imaginable style of music. A singer with a high soprano launched an assault on *Wuthering Heights* by Kate Bush. Further on, a string quartet drearily ran through a list of Viennese and Russian standards.

It was the second time John Ball found himself in Saint Petersburg. The first had been about four years back, maybe five. He found it hard to remember. It had been springtime and he'd stayed only two days. It was to attend a conference on Linear Algebra organized by the famous Steklov Institute. He told himself it would be nice to come back in winter, when the waters of the Neva were trapped in ice. From where he was standing, he could cross the river and arrive at the Peter and Paul Fortress with its Imperial tombs. He conjured the hurried footsteps of residents; he imagined them navigating streets strafed by glacial winds, bundled in thick coats and fur hats; he pictured the low-hanging sky and the wan light of public streetlamps drowned out by the almost perpetual night. Saint Petersburg is a city whose soul is laid bare only at midwinter. London's is unveiled only in pea-soup fog, Bergen's in the driving rain. And that of Rome appears in the blistering sunshine. Only Paris has a different soul for every passing season.

John Ball sat down at the terrace of a restaurant along the Moyka. The cloths covering its tables were a blue-and-green checked pattern. He noted bottles of chilled white wine in ice buckets, which waiters in starched shirts hurried back and forth pouring. "Must be a good spot," he thought to himself. He preferred on the whole to trust his instinct, rather than rely on tourist guides. And he had all evening to enjoy the role of a globe-trotting man of the world. He could stroll along the river banks, sip a few glasses of Caucasus wine and soak up the very soul of the universe, which hung palpably in the cool air of this fine summer night. The urge to wander took hold of him. John Ball was not just a world-class academic. A true Epicurean, he could savor all of life's pleasures. "A bit of a stroll it is," he told himself. "Besides, the time difference will keep me up for a few hours longer in any event."

Frankly, though, his heart wasn't in it. His mind turned over ugly thoughts that spoiled his enjoyment of the evening, lovely though it was. Over and over, he recalled his discipline's hearsay and gossip, the pettiness of inconsequential mathematicians, the jealousy of mediocre ones, the arrogance of its soaring eagles. The minor contingencies, unworthy of his field's pure essence, were making a mess of the festivities, his festivities. In a few short weeks—August 22nd to be precise—he was to stand proudly next to the King of Spain in the stately ballroom of a grand hotel in Madrid as the latter distributed the Fields Medal to four unquestionably deserving laureates. One of these mathematicians was to be Grigori Perelman. Following the Congress, John Ball would hang up his hat as President of the organization that brings together all of the world's mathematicians. He hoped it would be with the satisfaction of a job well done, and his tithe of glory... This most sacred mass of the intellect was held just once every four years—like the Olympics, he mused, except that there was just one competition, in a single discipline—and he categorically refused to see it tarnished with suspicion, machinations or seedy theatrics.

At the origin of these silent ripples, the epicenter of this agitation, invisible to outsiders, was a man. A man who jeopardized the fragile peace of this unobtrusive community. Not by any means a malicious troublemaker, an epic traitor, a pervert or even a cynic.

None of that. In fact, nothing could really be called his fault. And yet, he was the very crux of the problem.

And his name was Grigori Perelman. In exactly three days, on June 13th, he would turn forty years old. He would not be celebrating the event. Nor would he bring together family and friends. In any case, he had few of either. He would not pop the cork on a bottle of sparkling wine, French Champagne or otherwise. He would not be blowing out the candles on a birthday cake. He would merely register the fact. At most, he might take a few moments to think deeply about it. Forty years on planet Earth... Forty is precisely the age limit for receiving the Fields Medal, the single highest honor a mathematician can achieve. The equivalent of a Nobel Prize, since there is none for the discipline. It is said that Alfred Nobel purposefully left out mathematics from his list of prizes in order to avoid having to award it to a great mathematician of the time who happened also to be his wife's lover. For him, it would seem, merit ended at the bedroom door. True or not, the Nobel prize continues to ignore mathematics and mathematicians.

The latter minded very little. Contrary to the Nobel, which tends to reward success in terms of hours clocked, it's fair to say that mathematicians pay fair honor to youth, and don't consider grey hair or wrinkles a prerequisite in recognizing their greatest progeny. Grigori Perelman was indubitably one of these. He deserved the prize, perhaps more than any mathematician before him. Was it not Grigori Perelman who had solved one of the most longstanding and difficult problems known to topology? An immovable wall his peers had hurled themselves against for over a century? Some to the point of folly? More than that, hadn't he broken open a legend, a myth, a philosophical quest that went well beyond numbers and concepts, brought to light questions that touch on humankind and its place in the world? Was it not a dream to understand the shape of the universe? The Poincaré Conjecture? What?

When it became clear that Grigori Perelman would refuse to travel to Madrid to receive the medal intended for him, the upper echelons of mathematics, to put it bluntly, panicked. An announcement that the Fields Medal was to be bestowed on the extraordinary Russian academic was in no way business as usual. For the first time, a mathematician was becoming a public personality, a media darling, a popular icon. The number of people capable of understanding his demonstration might be counted on your fingers, but the Conjecture was such a historic problem, and its symbolic force was so powerful, that journalists all over the world had seized on the topic. Suddenly, the triumph over Poincaré's Conjecture was the property of humanity writ large. Also, the figure of Perelman itself was a source of interest to the media. There was his general air of mad genius—his unkempt beard, long hair and bushy eyebrows, his strikingly clear, somewhat disturbing gaze and his mismatched, worn clothing... There were also the stories and rumors, not all of them charitable. These were always told in whispers: his bouts of fury, his compulsions, his obsessions. Everything, in fact, that constituted the legend of Perelman. The myth of a sort of autistic extraterrestrial whose superhuman intelligence had picked the lock on a divine portal of knowledge.

As a result, the primary leadership of the International Mathematical Union met for a crisis summit at the organization's headquarters in Berlin. This had been the last weekend in May, three months before the Congress was to start. The permanent secretariat of the Union had moved to an office on the Markgrafenstrasse five years before, after Berlin won out over rival candidates Toronto and Rio de Janeiro. The East Berlin neighborhood it was in had been entirely rebuilt after reunification and remained somewhat soulless. Its uncompromising grid of streets, long, straight avenues and buildings in no particular style that all looked alike left an impression of rigid conformity at odds with the frenetic cultural activity that animated the rest of the German capital teeming with artist squats and street-art covered walls. It was a bit as though mathematicians had chosen to inhabit the most conservative and depressing side of modernity.

The atmosphere was heavy as the meeting was called to order. There were about a dozen of them around the table, all with suitably somber miens.

"We must convince Perelman to come to Madrid," said the Secretary-General. "We must," he stressed again.

All eyes had turned to John Ball, sitting at the head of the table, or perhaps the foot. As usual, he was wearing honey-colored corduroy trousers and a checked flannel shirt with the two top buttons undone. He sat with his legs crossed and a petulant expression on his face. He already knew what his colleagues expected of him. He made a feeble attempt to head off his peers.

"Gentlemen, I am a mathematician, not a diplomat," he ventured after a moment.

"With all due respect to both professions, I believe we require neither," answered a member of the proceedings who looked like a hermit sage. "The matter calls more for a mage or a prophet, I would say. Nothing short of a miracle could change the mind of that pigheaded Perelman."

Half an hour later, the details of his trip had been hammered out. John Ball would head to Saint Petersburg the very next week and speak with the obstinate Russian mathematician. He had carte blanche to indulge Grigori Perelman's every whim.

A few days before his departure, however, John Ball's mission took an unexpected turn. An unforeseen occurrence half a world away made it even more important—if such a thing were possible—that he succeed. The peaceable kingdom of mathematics had just been rocked by a seismic wave. The epicenter of this catastrophe lay in China. The tremors, though, were likely to be felt in Madrid. It had all started on June 6th, in the hushed surroundings of a conference hall in Beijing, as an offshoot of a seminar devoted to a recent branch of mathematics known as String Theory. It was six o'clock and the participants were wrapping up. The organizers had called a press conference. In a small lecture hall, Shing-Tung Yau was about to speak. It must be added here that in Beijing, professor Yau was a star, an emblematic figure of Chinese mathematics. From the very start of his career he had ceaselessly encouraged the training of young Chinese academics. He had spared no pains in hoisting the Middle Kingdom and its universities to the highest levels of his discipline.

The wait was prolonged. Journalists asked themselves why they had been asked to attend. But they were not to be disappointed. Shing-Tung finally took the stage. He administered thanks, drawing out the suspense. He then announced that two of his students, the researchers Cao and Zhu, had arrived at a full and definitive proof of the Poincaré Conjecture. Applause broke out. Yau dished the details. He explained that Grigori Perelman had, indeed achieved a tremendous feat, resting on the foundations provided by Richard Hamilton, but that his articles included certain shortcuts and lacunae and perhaps even errors. A vital pediment was missing. This stone had finally been placed, completing a monument of mathematics. Yau went so far as to offer a breakdown of the parties' relative contributions. He attributed half of the collective achievement to Hamilton, twenty percent to Perelman and thirty percent to Cao and Zhu! He went on to praise China's math program, emphasizing its tremendous progress, which in the past twenty years had made possible this accomplishment.

This surprise announcement had arrived precisely as the scientific community, following four years of scrupulous verifications, had finally agreed to credit Perelman for proving the Conjecture and just as the committee responsible for distributing the Fields Medal had decided to recognize this achievement by awarding it to the Russian. The whole house of cards had suddenly threatened to topple. It had nearly been the celebration of an eccentric mathematical genius who had spent the better part of his life struggling with the Conjecture as though it were a thousand-headed hydra, an epic hero-mathematician whose life would make the nightly news. Instead, there loomed a sordid accounting project to meanly dole out the shares of value for work that few human beings could comprehend.

The shadow of this lost opportunity made John Ball gnash his teeth. He finished his dinner more quickly than he would have liked and waved away the dessert menu. Taking another swallow of the French wine he had ordered—a Chateauneuf-du-Pape, definitely his favorite—he called for the check and paid. On the way back to his hotel, he lingered a moment in front of the Bronze Horseman, bathed in moonlight. In a murmur, he recited the few lines he could remember of Pushkin's eponymous poem.

> *Oh act of Peter, I'm in love*
> *With your strict and structured form,*
> *the Neva's commanding flow,*
> *Its granite banks, the design*
> *in the iron railings, the translucent dusk*
> *And moonless sheen*
> *Of dream-soaked nights.*

He gave up on strolling along the Neva. His mind gave him no peace. He needed sleep in order to focus on the task ahead.

"I am no Peter the Great," he reflected.

June 11, 2006, morning

The day of reckoning arrived. Reviving from its abbreviated night, the sun shone tremulously. John Ball waited. As usual, he was early, despite the time change and a lack of sleep. As far back as he could remember, he had never missed a significant appointment, whether disagreeable or pleasant. The only thing he despised more than waiting was making someone wait. The meeting was to take place at a magnificent palace overlooking the Neva, a textbook case of Neoclassical style in late 18th-century Russia. Here too, the façade had recently received a facelift, as had a majority of the city center's historic buildings. The white-painted columns and pediment contrasted smartly with the pinkish tones of the walls. Nice workmanship. John Ball paced the quay before the building once more, then decided to go inside. The foyer was huge and austere. A young receptionist with magnificent golden hair falling down to her shoulders came to his aid. After asking his name, she indicated the main staircase. A small room overlooking the river on the floor above had been reserved in the British mathematician's name. A discreet wooden sign was hung on the door. Inside, a modern, rectangular table set about with four chairs occupied the center of the room. On it were two glasses and a bottle of French mineral water. These functional furnishings clashed with the ornate moldings of the ceiling, the elegant crystal chandelier and the great silk rug that all but hid the room's oak flooring. For a moment the Englishman's mind wandered, rifling through everything he'd ever learned about Russian history from Peter the Great to Nicolas II. Would he have time to visit the Hermitage Museum tomorrow? He'd so much like to go back and see the display of legendary Fabergé eggs.

The site of their meeting had to be kept an absolute secret. With the Congress in Madrid mere weeks away, it was crucial to avoid any sign that would provide a clue as to the future recipients of the Fields Medal. The laureates were to be announced with great pomp and circumstance by John Ball in Madrid with the King of Spain standing by. Thousands of mathematicians and hundreds of journalists from all over the world would be in attendance. Any leak, even the slightest, would completely destroy the suspense so necessary to the event's success. John Ball, well used to the untrammeled creativity of British bookmakers capable of organizing bets on practically anything from sporting events to elections at the House of Commons to say nothing of divorces among the Royals, wondered if the Union's list of medalists would excite such fervor. Why not? Nothing was beyond them, the name of the next Pope, rainfall on the Scandinavian peninsula next year, you name it. He doubted it though, somehow. Mathematicians as a caste are hardly fascinating to the masses.

He recalled one of his mathematician friends who used to begin every public appearance by recounting how proud he was to be a "mathematician" until one time at a trendy bar in Mayfair a girl for whom he'd bought a drink asked him what he did for a living. The bewilderment registered on her face at his answer dashed his illusions. Since then, he claimed, he had limited his reply to saying he was a university professor. When he was feeling up to it, he would go for musician, or artist. Mathematicians intimidated girls and failed to interest bookmakers. Ball chided himself for having smiled when he'd listened to this sexist story. But the bottom line remained—all his elaborate precautions for keeping this interview top-secret were probably unnecessary.

John Ball had phoned Grigori Perelman the week before, somewhat apprehensively. He was worried the latter might refuse to see him. To be fair, the stories in circulation about the Russian's angry outbursts were enough to deter the bravest of men. Luckily, he had had to make do with the mother. While pacing the room along the window side to pass the time, he smiled to himself, imagining the scene. Grigori, in slippers, seated before the small round table in the living room where he sometimes worked, the curtains drawn, the television silenced. The only light would have come from the yellowing shade of a floor lamp in the corner, but it would suffice to light up the man's face, like a Caravaggio painting. The mother would have been busy in the narrow kitchen of the State-issued apartment she had occupied for the last twenty years. The radio would have been dispensing classical music, perhaps a violin concerto by Tchaikovsky, or an opera. Grigori was immensely fond of the great soprano arias, those by Puccini especially. He frequented the Saint Petersburg opera regularly, always seated in the cheap nosebleed seats up top. The telephone had rung. It was Lubov Lvovna who answered, right after the second ring. Not to appear negligent, she asked: "Would you like to speak to Grigori?" knowing full well that it was pointless to hand him the phone. He loathes speaking to someone he cannot see. She had therefore acted as the intermediary. In broken English delivered with a strong Slavic accent, she begged his pardon, breaking off several times to address Grigori in Russian: Would he like to see Mr. Ball? She excused herself again, then, more firmly, provided the date and time for them to rendezvous.

But who was she, really? A tender and protective mother? The multitasking assistant of an autistic genius? The Svengali of an artist at the height of his powers? Hypotheses tumbled around John Ball's mind, with none coming up a clear winner. He had no idea.

There was a knock at the door. With some difficulty, John pulled out of his reverie. The young woman with the blond hair reappeared, smiling this time. John was reminded of a painting by Moïse Kisling he had recently chanced on at the Petit Palais in Geneva, *Young girl with braids*. The Russian girl's tresses were as blond as Kisling's model had been jet black. "Beauty adapts to the material at hand," he mused. Grigori Perelman was standing right behind the hostess. He was a good head taller. The young lady announced the new arrival solemnly, as one might give the name of a distinguished visitor at a gala affair. The door closed behind Grigori. The waiting was over. The lions had been unleashed. Let the fight begin.

Perelman possessed the physique of an Old Testament prophet. Except that destiny, in a moment of distraction, had mixed in a bit of Norse deity. His pale blue eyes shone out from amidst a tangle of capillary excess that appeared to have no other function than to protect the two azure windows like a treasure buried in a rainforest clearing. Like the rest of his hair, his bushy eyebrows were an indeterminate shade between chestnut and red. They hung like giant quotation marks around his eyes, meeting at the bridge of the nose. The rest of his face was occupied by a beard that covered even his upper lip. Long curling locks fell down haphazardly to each side of his face, though tucked behind his ears. They were not without recalling the curlicues affected by Orthodox Jews from Eastern Europe. Only the top of his skull was bald, giving the impression of a smooth and endless forehead.

This face, that of a hermit or sage depending on your perspective, seemed tenuously balanced atop a gigantic body. John Ball was impressed. It was not the first time he had met the Russian mathematician, but today he appeared taller and more massive than he had in memory. The circumstances of their meeting merely amplified these feelings. The two were so close that he could physically sense Perelman's aura.

The meeting began like any other one-on-one meeting of professionals, engineers or management types. They sat facing each other, casually leaning back in their chairs. Perelman crossed his legs. Ball filled two glasses of water and handed one to his guest. The latter inquired politely how the visitor's trip had been, what hotel he was at, and if he was tired. From there, the conversation moved on to other trivial topics. Ball enthused about the unique atmosphere of the city during the White Nights Festival, praising the newly regained beauty of the Tsar's capital. Perelman explained how the city had succeeded in financing the refurbishment of its historic buildings thanks to revenues from tourism. At last, their exchange trickled towards the international event coming up in a few short weeks that would make Saint Petersburg the center of the world.

"The G8 summit is in a month, isn't it?"

"Yes, mid-July I believe, but you might say the circus was already in town. These last few days, the city has been riled up. More police on the streets. Military boats moving discreetly along the river. Even the dockworkers are nervous. I have no idea why. You can't see it, of course, since you have no frame of reference, but to anyone who lives here, it's obvious."

"Where will the heads of State be gathering? Not in the city center, surely?"

"No, they've selected a small town that faces the Gulf of Finland. Strelna, it's called. About ten miles from Saint Petersburg. My mother took me there several times when I was little. Peter the Great had a palace built there, but he hardly ever used it. He liked the Peterhof better. Further away from town. Later on, the property belonged to the Archduke Constantin Pavlovich, that's why it's called the Constantine palace. A handsome chateau, huge French formal gardens, complete with a canal, fountains and waterworks. It was a first—and failed, naturally—attempt to copy Versailles. Then the buildings were practically destroyed by German bombs during WWII. For a long time, the ruins just sat around. No one was interested in it. That's how I remember it. Then, about five years ago, Vladimir Putin decided to have it renovated. Now it's one of the presidential residences."

"A new palace for a new Tsar. Or so his critics might say. I didn't know you were so interested in politics."

"Politics? You misunderstand me. I am not interested in politics. I have no idea what topics the heads of the so-called great powers will be addressing next month. And frankly, I couldn't care less. I am a passionate student of history though. What is history if not a flux, with hollows and bulges, accidents, fissures, accelerations and pauses? I enjoy following its course in thought, letting its dynamics take over my mind. It always brings me back to my mathematical research. And frankly, just between us, John, could there really be any better place than Russia to do that? Russia fell out of History for decades. Communists believed they'd dealt a death blow to that pesky determinism. That's what I learned at University in my mandatory classes on Marxism, dialectics and scientific materialism. I see where Putin is coming from. Bringing together world leaders in a palace of the Tsars. Isn't it a wonderful way of healing that wound and committing the Russian soul to the soothing current of history once more?"

"You didn't really have all those classes, did you?"

"I did. Back when I studied at the University in Leningrad, as it was called at the time. The faculty's math department was at Petrodvorets, maybe 20 miles from the city. I took the train every day. It was grueling. Classes on Marxism were still dispensed from the main buildings in Leningrad proper. I remember another class we had, called *Critique of contemporary bourgeois thought and anti-communist ideology*. Quite a program, huh? I didn't miss a single class. Surprised? I realized pretty quickly that there was meaning there to be found. If, and only if, you despised politics."

"Surely, you want to know what they're going to talk about? I read in an English paper this morning that the summit would focus on energy issues. Also, nuclear arms proliferation and education. It would seem that education is a big topic with Putin."

"Why not? Education is a good topic. I was lucky to study at a time when the excellence of academia was a matter of national sovereignty. Times have changed. Whatever. I think I can safely say they're unlikely to discuss topology at any rate."

Grigori Perelman had delivered his last remark without so much as a smile. His voice had not changed one iota, but continued in the same monotone with which he had spoken of Russian history. It was almost as though the man couldn't tell when he was being funny.

It was now close on an hour that the two men had been amiably exchanging pleasantries. John Ball suddenly felt tired, as though he were trapped in a moment of burdensome nothingness. The time flowing by them was taking them nowhere. His patience was wearing thin. There was no way he'd hold out an entire day at this pace. His blood boiled. He could feel the artery in his neck beat like it would at the height of a tennis match. Just like a long exchange of back-court volleys on wet clay. The two men had sagely retreated to their baselines. They batted the ball back and forth, careful of their effects, waiting for the other to commit an unforced error. It was not a style of play John enjoyed. He liked to fight his battles up front. His preference was for short, hard attacks that could only end in death or dishonor.

He stood up abruptly and shrugged his shoulders to lessen the pain in his back that had bothered him since he woke up. He headed towards the wide bay windows outlined behind the heavy cotton drapes and pushed a panel aside. Outside, activity had swelled in the street and on the river. A small herd of tourists milled around in front of the building. A few yards further on, a heavyset, young women, probably their guide, waved a furled umbrella to ensure visibility. Ball found it amusing. An umbrella. Meanwhile the sun was shining brightly in the sky over Saint Petersburg.

It was time to change strategies. The observation phase is over, he told himself. Turning back around like a leopard ready to leap on its prey, he was struck by the scene confronting him. Perelman sat like a schoolboy in detention, his elbows on the table. His right hand calmly stroked his beard as he looked up with the quizzical, innocent air of a child waiting to hear the rest of a story.

John Ball was overcome, touched, vulnerable. No longer a savage hunter, he found himself suddenly an antelope that had stumbled. He needed to regroup and muster his patience. There was a long day ahead, and there remained all of the next day for him to succeed. This was not a battle he could win in a single move.

As he had readied himself for their meeting that very morning, John Ball promised himself that he would lose no time in broaching the topic of his visit. Before leaving, he'd had a discussion with a psychiatrist friend at Cambridge who had studied the "Perelman case" among many other more or less autistic scientists. This had left him convinced that the best approach was to be firm, frank and spontaneous. Better to avoid convoluted phrasing, digressions and subtle suggestions. His best bet was to address Perelman directly, unambiguously and to present the issue as a dichotomy. As he'd walked from the hotel to the meeting, Ball had repeated to himself: "I will tell Grigori Perelman that he must come to Madrid to receive the Fields Medal, because his peers have determined that he deserves this recognition. Simple, really."

John Ball sat down again in front his Russian counterpart. He took a deep breath, then emptied his lungs. Just as he would during a meditation session. His breathing naturally reasserted its rhythm. The tennis metaphor bounced back into his mind. He'll be serving with new balls, he thought. And with that, he finally dove in.

"My dear Grigori, it would be an immense pleasure to enjoy spending two days—or more—chatting with you about the destiny of Mother Russia and its irruption into the history of the 20th century. So if you don't mind, let's deal with the professional aspect of my visit at once. That way we can drop it. Especially since I am sure you have an idea why I'm here. In its great wisdom, the Board of Directors of the International Mathematical Union has asked me to come and invite you to receive the Fields Medal. It is unusual to make the announcement in advance of the Congress itself, but we know you rarely travel, and I wanted to personally make sure that you would be willing to make the journey to Madrid."

Perelman closed his eyes for a long moment before answering.

"My dear John, it's very kind of you, and I sincerely thank you for being so solicitous on my behalf. However, with all due respect, and despite my reluctance to contradict you, I believe your explanation is not quite accurate. If you are here today in Saint Petersburg at a time when the summer temperatures make your lovely English countryside so attractive, missing your family and the city of belfries, I somewhat doubt it is courtesy or gratitude that moved you. I rather believe that you are afraid."

"Afraid? What are you talking about? I must say I've not ever been called a coward before."

John Ball had jerked. His shock was by no means feigned. Perelman's change of tone had taken him by surprise. Well then, if he had expected a fight. Well, here it was.

"Oh dear, please don't misunderstand"—this time Perelman's response flew back like a ball hit straight from the rebound. "I wouldn't dream of insulting you. Please forgive me. You must have heard that I'm not especially gifted in the communication department. Sometimes, I just blunder along saying what I think. People aren't used to it. It's not you personally, John. I meant the institution you, rather imprudently perhaps, have accepted to preside over. This grand farce of universal mathematics. They are trembling with fear, aren't they? Admit it. They don't want the bearded eccentric from Saint Petersburg to make a mess of their great pow-wow at the altar of intelligence. The World Congress of Mathematicians must remain above controversy, smooth and pure, like a well-solved equation. You are the messenger of their fear."

"Alright then. At least that's out in the open. You have no intention of coming to Madrid, I assume, given your virulent reaction. But, if I am the emissary of fear, you hardly exude joyful serenity. I believe you are fighting the wrong battle, Grigori. Sometimes it is necessary to accept the homage proffered by your peers, even if you despise them. You should see in it, if not the full measure of your merits, an idea of your duties. You may wall yourself in solitude and remain deaf to praise, but that won't erase your debts."

"Come on. Don't go overboard John. You knew I would refuse to accept this prize. It wouldn't be the first time. I'm a known recidivist. Your rhetoric is lovely, but I find it a bit presumptuous that you thought you could change my mind. It's been said I'm a tough nut. It must be true. What really bothers me, though, is that I don't get just why you're making such a fuss over me. After all, I would hardly be the first mathematician to decline this trinket... I mean, medal."

"You're thinking of Grothendieck?"

"Yes, of course."

"There are certain commonalities between you."

"What do you mean? He was, I believe, bald."

John Ball smiled. After the unyielding exchanges the Englishman and Russian had just engaged in, the touch of wit was like a beam of light, a ray of hope. A chink in the armor.

Alexander Grothendieck had, in fact, refused the Fields Medal in 1966, the same year Grigori Perelman was born. That was one coincidence. But those were different times. A time of turmoil, where every level of society was rife with insubordination. Whether you were a politician or a philosopher, a musician or an academic, everyone felt they had to be something of a rebel. A little bit rock 'n roll. Grothendieck had been in tune with his era—defiant and mischievous.

Granted, the two mathematicians resembled each other not at all, physically speaking. Their careers, on the other hand, offered many similarities. Heredity, for one. Like Perelman, Grothendieck had a Russian Jewish father. And what a father he was! Sacha Schapiro's life read like a summary of the whole tragic 20th century. A militant anti-tsarist in Ukraine as a youth, he went on to distinguish himself with the Anarchist movement in Germany during the 1930s. He then joined up with Republican forces in Spain during the civil war, before taking refuge in France, fleeing the advancing franquista troops... All that, only to tumble out of the frying pan into the Nazi fire. Arrested, interned at Drancy, then deported, he had died at Auschwitz in 1942. Sixty years later, almost to the day, Grigori Perelman's father would finally emigrate to Israel, after years of struggle against the Communist regime. Another coincidence. While papa crisscrossed Europe battling fascisms, little Alexander remained hidden in the mountains of central France. Needless to say, he survived. After the war, he became a solitary adult. Like Perelman, he lived alone with his mother for a long time. Like Perelman would thirty years later, he withdrew from the world. In the early 1980s in his case. Breaking off all ties with academia, he lived alone as a recluse near a small village in the Pyrenees. Many considered Alexander Grothendieck to be the greatest mathematician of the 20th century. His research in the area of logic had founded an entire new branch of geometry. Like Grigori Perelman, he had obviously deserved the Fields Medal.

"True, he was bald from a young age," answered Ball, falling in with the joke to lighten the atmosphere. "Do you know what he said in his letter refusing the Crafoord prize?"

"No. I didn't even know he'd refused the Crafoord. So, he was a recidivist too!"

"I figured you would bring up Grothendieck. So I went over his biography on the plane. That's were I ran into the letter. A sharp nib, indeed. How about: 'The ethics prevailing in the scientific community (at least among mathematicians) are now so degraded that outright theft among colleagues has virtually become the law of the land.' What say you to that, eh?"

"Did he really write that?"

"Unbelievable, isn't it? The whole letter is incendiary. How about this sentence: 'Accepting a role in the game of prizes and awards would mean consecrating an attitude and evolution that I recognize as deeply unhealthy.' "

"A devious mind."

"Or a free spirit?"

"If you say so. I'm afraid I'll be something of a disappointment by comparison. In my case, refusal means nothing beyond my refusing. To borrow Grothendieck's vocabulary, my 'no' is *autological*. I'm asking you, John. I'm begging you, please don't try and give it a political, philosophical, or even a scientific dimension. It would make you no better than the apparatchiks who distribute these baubles without understanding a damn word of the work they are rewarding."

"Alright then, you have nothing in common with Grothendieck. But in that case, it's pointless for you to use him as an alibi or an example," answered John Ball with a triumphant smile. "There's the answer to your question, Grigori: 'why are we making such a fuss about you?' It's because your refusal isn't meaningful like his."

"Point taken. You're right, John, I have nothing in common with that chattering, militant anarchist agitator."

"I have a confession. I would never have sacrificed two days of family time to convince Grothendieck of anything. But you're different. You're not a radical," John Ball concluded with a broad smile, proud to have scored even a small victory.

The British mathematician had used a trick. He had succeeded in throwing off the precisely calibrated gears of Perelman's mind with a mere grain of sand. He made a sneaky attempt to push his advantage.

"There's another sentence Grothendieck wrote that you might identify with more. Something like 'The true measure of fruition is progeny, not honors.' What if you used this comedy of honors to deliver a legacy?"

This time, Perelman reacted, visibly irritated. What on Earth was the point of this semantic game Ball was forcing on him? His shoulders trembled, he squirmed. His gestures became discombobulated. His answer came in bursts, like fire from a damaged machine gun.

"I'm not interested in honors. And I don't need progeny either. 'Fruition' is *not* my thing. Posterity neither. I'm looking for truth. The history of mathematics can grind to a halt tomorrow as far as I'm concerned. Forever. It makes no difference to me."

"You're missing the point, Grigori. You respect your mentors too much not to believe in some kind of intellectual heredity, a mathematical filiation. History isn't over, and that goes for mathematics as well. What would Alexandrov think if he heard you now?"

The question Ball had asked was purposefully treacherous. He knew well how significant Alexandrov had been to Perelman's career. Grigori was the last doctoral student the great Russian geometer had accepted; at a time when he was already well on in years. The younger man would go on to become a specialist of the famous "Alexandrov spaces," which is what first earned him a name in the tight-knit world of topologists. But the relationship between student and master was not limited to math. Alexander Alexandrov had influenced Perelman profoundly as a man. The elder's intransigence, moral principles, his uncompromising conception of honesty, his loyalty toward the Soviet regime and the strength he had shown in combating its failings, his passion for mountain-climbing... all these had combined to form a mythical Alexandrov that occupied Perelman's personal pantheon.

His shot landed, a well-aimed ball. Grigori remained silent. He rocked back and forth on his chair, smoothing out the creases of his pants over his thigh with his right hand. John even thought he caught a sort of humming, as though the Russian were singing into his beard. Left without an answer, Ball went on, determined to go for the jugular.

"You underestimate reality, Grigori. You can't withdraw from the ubiquitous trade in symbols just by refusing honors or recognition. So you decline to be an iconic figure of mathematics? Fine. You'll find yourself stuck with some other halo instead. You'll become the hero of the meek. More likely, you'll be an aspiration for half-assed revolutionaries. In fact, just yesterday, I was fishing around on an internet discussion forum and found this." Here, John Ball removed from his vest pocket a wrinkled piece of paper on which he had scribbled a few sentences and proceeded to read: "'It's just so great to see that there are still a some brave and more highly-evolved people out there who can think for themselves without looking at everything through the prism of money, standing up to the capitalist ideology we've been spoon-fed for decades.' That's the stuff they're already writing about Grigori Perelman. What do you think? Are you feeling up to the task of providing a bulwark against capitalism? Wouldn't you be better off bowing your head for a second on the podium to let us hang a medal around your neck?"

"Don't worry, John. They'll forget me. The humble ones, and the revolutionaries too. I will be so silent—or so unpleasant—that they'll get tired of knocking on my door. You'll see. They'll have no trouble finding more exciting heroes. The medal comes with inconvenient baggage: posterity.

"Posterity isn't an opt-in clause, you know. You are part of history whether you like it or not."

The curtain fell heavily, closing the first act. Ball had lost the battle and he knew it. Despite Grothendieck. Despite Alexandrov. Despite his debating skills. His last salvo betrayed his annoyance. His interior monologue spun out of control. What beastly difference could it possibly make after all? If this temperamental Russian preferred to barricade himself in his miserable apartment instead of strutting around a room full of celebrities with a glass of champagne? Let him. He forced himself to calm down. There was no way he would convince Perelman of anything if he kept to a rational playing field. He had tried to solve the problem like a mathematician. That was a mistake. He wondered why the hell he'd ever accepted this hopeless task. At best, it was naive, at worst, it smacked of arrogance.

June 11, 2006, afternoon

"Let's go for a walk," announced Perelman. Without waiting for an answer, he stood up and headed for the door. John Ball hesitated a moment before following. What if they were recognized wandering about the city's streets? What if their confidential meeting was plastered across the front page of tomorrow's papers? Perelman turned around to stare at him with the same childish surprise Ball had witnessed earlier. "This paranoia is silly," he thought, "I'm behaving like some kind of secret agent afraid of blowing my cover. To hell with this absurd charade! It's idiotic to be so suspicious. No one gives a damn about the perambulations of two obscure mathematicians." He smiled internally, picturing spies in dark glasses lurking in strategic spots around the city. Just like the heyday of the Cold War. Probably poised to transmit messages in Morse code to their Chinese or American handlers. How on Earth had he convinced himself that his mission was so important? He felt a sudden need to reconnect with the world, to go back to basics. He wanted to leave this sterile bubble, so like the isolation wards reserved for victims of contagious disease.

Perhaps Perelman was right. Are not mathematics a golden key by which to enter the very body of the universe, to commune with nature and understand its rules—deciphering an infinitely complex score in order to fully experience the simplicity of its music? Is not the practice of mathematics a form of meditation, a quest for peace of mind, a means of focusing on the deep blue of the sky and ignoring the passing clouds? And what have we made of it, Ball asked himself—a timid, fretful bureaucracy, the sanctum of petty technicians.

"Indeed, an excellent idea," replied Ball.

Perelman already had an itinerary in mind—not that their outing was premeditated in any way—but the center of Saint Petersburg was his natural habitat. He was familiar with every single feature of its topography, from its broad prospects to its hidden-most shortcuts. He intended to first take his guest along the Palace Embankment to admire the façade of the Hermitage, but without going inside. The crush of tourists would already be too dense at this hour. He would tell Ball all about the collections, which he knew by heart, going from room to room, like one of those virtual museum tours you can do these days on your computer. Then they would head over to the enormous golden dome of Saint Isaac's Cathedral. On the way, he would suggest they sit for a while on a bench in the Alexander Garden, where the leafy trees conceal the façade of the Admiralty, a place he especially enjoyed for its shaded paths, at the end of which emerge stone busts of Gogol, Glinka and others. After that, they would stroll along the canals as far as the typically Russian Revival-style Church of the Savior on Spilled Blood, reminiscent of Saint Basile's Cathedral in Moscow. But, to begin with, they would have to cross one of the bridges over the Neva. The palace they were at was on the wrong bank.

Cities built along a river often have another side to them, a lesser bank, colonized as a spillover effect, a bank lacking distinguished historical antecedents. Sometimes it is the blue-collar bank, that of workers and fishermen. The side of immigrants, slaves and the poor. Or, on the contrary, it may be the serene preserve of aristocrats and priests. The name of these neighborhoods always betrays their tagalong nature. In Rome you have the *Trastavere*, "that which is beyond the Tiber." Florentines, for their part, refer to the city's left bank as the *Oltrarno*. Once again, Paris is the sole exception. Its two banks treat each other as equals. As rivals perhaps, the Left and the Right, the Bohemian and Bourgeois, striving for centuries to find favor with painters and poets. Saint Petersburg never succeeded in encompassing its waterway. Town and river cohabitate, its bridges discretely stepping over the current, but the Neva remains sovereign; never has it let its course be fettered by the city.

So off they went, the young woman in braids having bid them a ceremonious goodbye. Leaving the palace, they continued along the river to Trinity Square, where a pointed bell tower rises toward heaven at the center of the Peter and Paul Fortress. This is the river's widest point. The iron bridge spans the six hundred meters separating the two banks with a series of ten openwork arches in the Art Nouveau style. Perelman delivered an unceasing stream of commentary while continuing to walk at a brisk clip. He was like a sightseeing guide anxious to get through an overly ambitious program. He covered how construction of this monument extended from the 19th century to the early 20th, like a temporal bridge of sorts, its completion date coinciding with the city's 200th anniversary. He pointed out the beauty of the street lamps along the handsome metalwork parapet and so forth.

Arriving on the other bank, the Russian mathematician turned around and took a deep breath. Standing tall, the better to embrace the view of the fortress, his gaze swept over the imposing rostral columns in front of the stock exchange that evoked the wealth of ships entering the harbor. Off to the left lay the palace museums of Vasilevsky Island. He had always had a distinct preference for the view from this side of the river.

Was it the gentle breeze off the sea that drew Perelman's thoughts back to John Ball and his reason for being there? Was he even aware of the shift? With no intelligible transition, as though to distance himself from regret, the Russian returned to the topic of mathematics.

"I think I solved the Poincaré Conjecture as a form of relief, it was a problem that kept me from sleeping."

"I can't think of a better reason to work on a problem, but do you sleep so much better now?" asked Ball, who was relieved by the conversation's reversal.

"I don't suffer as much as I used to. You might say the obsession dissipated. Sleep comes more naturally when I lie down. It's when I wake up that I get anxious again, not every day, but sometimes. And it happens for no reason. It would seem that I've traded nightmares for the torments of the day. Sometimes the search for meaning is a torture all its own. How is it possible to accept that the most extraordinary demonstration imaginable may open onto so little in the way of new horizons? So it's definitely a sphere, and then what?"

"Isn't that the tragedy of all mathematicians? Our reasoning is so pure that we get drunk on it; we feel as though we hold the world in our hands. A logic so perfect it prompts an extraordinary sensation of almost absolute power over our surroundings, and an unwillingness to admit that it's ultimately an illusion. I think the real danger lies in letting our innocence become arrogance."

"A pretty turn of phrase," said Grigori. "You're probably right. Omnipotence is a fantasy we must relinquish. Actually, psychoanalysts claim that only the infant is all-powerful. The rest of our lives is nothing but a story of loss, a litany of renunciations, one after another."

"Are you interested in psychoanalysis as well?"

"In a way. What interests me is imperfection, all the imperfections we must gird ourselves to resolve, all the spaces needing to be filled. I like the idea of mending, churning, remodeling. Those are processes common to most of the sciences, actually. Take psychoanalysis, is it not a topology of consciousness, a patient mapping of our mental fissures?"

"Fissures that yawn wider and wider with time, to the tune of loss and renunciation. Where do you stand today? Have you said goodbye to understanding everything?"

"Not yet, I'm afraid. I have only learned to distance myself from the madding crowd."

"You are still possessed by the demon of Mathematics, my dear Grigori. Time will tell!"

The conversation continued along these lines, as unpredictable and disjointed as the route they followed appeared mapped and structured by Perelman. Like a pendulum, the Russian's speech swung at times into the past. From there, he would would conjure vivid recollections, rich with biographical details. Other times he moved into an imaginary world where abstraction fought tooth and nail with the real. Then suddenly, some gravitational force would draw the discussion back to the here and now. Eschewing the straight line, and knowing better than anyone that the shortest path between two points is that which avoids pitfalls, Perelman coaxed his colleague into twists and turns that owed nothing to chance. They passed through the French-style parterres of the Summer Garden, walked along the Swan Canal, then crossed the Moyka to the most eclectic of Mikhailovsky's gardens, a subtle blend of Cartesian geometry and bucolic groves.

By the side of the way on one of the central paths, two stools sat on opposite sides of an iron folding table that clashed horribly with the surroundings. There, two elderly gentlemen sat playing chess. The one behind the light-colored pieces looked every bit the scion of some White Russian family. He cut quite a figure with his straight-backed, aristocratic bearing, his clear gaze and refined mustache. His shirt was buttoned to the collar, where it met a carefully knotted silk scarf. His partner, on the other hand, was frail and almost bald. Swathed in a jacquard cardigan with an unfortunate color scheme, he wore small wire-rimmed spectacles. A pair of bushy black eyebrows offered a glimpse of what his face must have looked like as a handsome dark-haired youth, but only a trace.

John Ball sidled up to the table discreetly. A swift glance at the chessboard was enough for him to anticipate the outcome. Black held a strategic advantage. However invisible to the untutored, it left little hope for his opponent.

"Do you play chess?" asked Perelman, who had caught the gleam in the Englishman's eye.

"From time to time, yes, but I played much more when I was young. Now, I prefer to watch my friends play. I find I'm better at analyzing other people's matches."

"An occupational hazard of being a mathematician. The chessboard and rules of the game make for a very rich topological space, don't you think?"

"Do you know what Marcel Duchamp used to say? The French avant-garde artist, I mean?" asked John Ball.

"No, I don't. I do, however, very much like his great Cubist picture, *Portrait of Chess Players*. I had an opportunity to see it at the Pompidou Museum in Paris a few years ago. If I recall rightly, it's a very dark painting showing a game between his two brothers."

"Exactly. Jacques and Raymond. Duchamp was an inveterate chess player. He said, 'There is more beauty in a game of chess than in mathematics. It is a more visual beauty than that of mathematics, it takes a physical form'. And I agree with him! You cannot reduce the game of chess to a mathematical representation, even an exercise in topology."

"And I might answer you," responded Perelman, "that, as a matter of fact, I go to great lengths to give physical form to my mathematical concepts, so much so that I sometimes feel I come close to a tangible beauty of sorts. But, let it stand. The artist often has the clearer sight."

"It's been said that you're a chess wizard. Is that so?"

"A great many things less true have been said about me. It was my father who taught me to play. My father was very proud of me. Always. Each time he turned up a new book on chess pawing through stalls of used books, he would buy it as a present for me. Especially if it contained chess problems or analysis of games by Grand Masters. He used to bring me lots of books, treatises on mathematics or physics mostly. Every evening, he would set me new logic problems to solve. Since I almost always succeeded, he was very proud of me, as I told you already, but I believe that what made him most proud, more than anything, was when I succeeded in beating him at chess. In fact, it probably prevented him from playing his best and reduced my merit accordingly. Later on, I took a chess course my teacher Valery Ryzhik used to run one evening a week after class. He too believed I had a great talent for chess.

"Did you think so as well?"

"No, I was like you, I preferred to commentate on other people's matches. One day, my father came home smiling broadly. Before he had even taken off his coat or greeted my mother and sister, he lunged at me brandishing a tattered pamphlet. The little book contained the blow by blow of a match between Albert Einstein and Robert Oppenheimer which, as legend has it, took place at

Princeton University in 1933. Einstein drew White and played a Spanish opening. We spent hours going over each move until we were forced to admit its importance was more historical than theoretical.

In the park, the slight, bald man had shifted to the offensive. The face of the old aristocrat tightened, his shoulders hunched imperceptibly and his breathing quickened as his eyes narrowed, his wrinkled hands trembling slightly under the table. His entire body seemed to be steeling for the inevitable defeat. It was clear that this was a customary outcome.

John Ball was compelled to recognize that notwithstanding all his efforts to remain at a distance intellectually, he was impressed with Perelman. Despite the man's uncertain diction and vagaries of speech, despite the lulls that left yawning chasms in his delivery, despite what was visible of his unspoken fears and deep resentment, the Russian's conversation was more than pleasant, it was captivating.

Perelman displayed tremendous erudition, a real ability to knit together seemingly disparate subjects with great cultural depth; yet, even if he managed for moments at a time to embrace the entire world in his mind, he was inexorably drawn back to his obsessions, to his endless quest for the slightest imperfections. He broached the topic of art and touched on politics. He discussed science and games alike. History and the local weather. Building systems. While Ball delighted in sharing his emotions, Perelman reeled off facts, figures, dates, lining up causes and effects. He moved about, without ever a misstep, in a labyrinth of his own making. People tended to think he was trying to awe his audience and show off his knowledge or display some kind of intellectual superiority. Ball grasped that Perelman would be utterly incapable of experiencing anything like condescension. His mind simply worked differently from that of other people. The mechanics of things were obvious to him; it obscured the mechanics of the soul.

The performance continued. The two protagonists were alone on stage, with only posterity looking on. After this relative lull, the action picked up again. The scenery rolled away. The plot took over. The only element missing was a suggestive drum roll. In a slow-motion sequence worthy of a Constructivist painting, John Ball reached into his jacket pocket and removed a sheet of paper carefully folded in quarters. It was the famous dispatch from the People's Daily Press Agency a few days earlier. Western media hadn't yet broken the story, so there was little chance that the few Russian publications interested in mathematics had done so. Ball unfolded this paper, ran his hands over its surface several times in order to remove the creases, and handed it to Perelman. The latter scanned it in a few seconds before looking up at the Englishman. "So what?" he seemed to ask.

"You don't seem surprised. You knew already, didn't you?" said John, making a play for complicity.

"Yes, of course. For reasons that are beyond me, I have several friends who are passionate about tracking down any scrap of information that relates to my work. They watch and wait, peruse and pluck. Then they report. They're my watchdogs."

"I see. Does that make friendship the tie that binds you to the world?"

"Probably."

"Well then, what do you think of it? Did you notice that odd sentence in the abstract? 'This proof should be taken as the crowning element of the Hamilton-Perelman theory of Ricci flows.' Have you ever seen anything so arrogant in a scientific publication? What kind of ethics can you expect of mathematicians who congratulate themselves for their discovery in their own paper? After all, shouldn't one wait for one's peers to attribute merit to a piece of work? Why the emphasis? And what about 'crowning'? A ridiculous word that's completely out of place in a research paper. Ball had fired off these questions in a feverish tone, rapidly, as though squeezing off rounds with a Kalashnikov.

"You ask these questions like they're rhetorical, John. But, honestly, do you know how to say 'crowning' in Chinese? Can you say for certain that you understand the language and its subtleties? You are looking at this event through the lens of an Oxford University Professor, which you are, with all the assumptions and deformations that entails. For my part, I know that Shing-Tung Yau is a great mathematician."

"No one claims otherwise."

"I don't know professors Cao or Zhu personally. They are students of Yau's and haven't published much, but Shing-Tung Yau is a great mathematician." Perelman repeated the phrase as though he hadn't heard John Ball's reply.

"That's not the point, Grigori," Ball shot back, annoyed. "These two Chinese mathematicians, who are, as you point out, not well-known, claim to have identified 'holes' or 'cracks' in your reasoning. They've announced, rather arrogantly, that they've brought the Poincaré Conjecture to a definitive close. You can't just ignore this news."

"I'm not ignoring it. It's a fact. It's impossible to ignore a matter of public record. What more can I say? I don't know Cao or Zhu. Professor Yau is a highly respected academic guarantor. His work on differential geometry and on Calabi-Yau manifolds has made critical advances."

"I know all that. He received the Fields Medal on the strength of those results. And, I might add, *he* at least did not for one second make a fuss about coming to collect his prize. But that's not the issue. The question is, is the word of the celebrated Professor Yau validating this research enough to say that Cao and Zhu did find cracks in your reasoning?"

Perelman's shell was breaking up under the Englishman's repeated onslaughts.

"I've only read the abstract of their paper," he admitted, relenting. "The full publication hasn't been released yet. Or, at least, I haven't received it. The holes they speak of are not obvious to me. They claim my demonstration is difficult to follow. I'm sure they're right. If it had been simple to understand, maybe it would have been easier to come up with."

John Ball did not seem to have caught the whiff of bitter irony in Perelman's last sentence. He soldiered on.

"The topologists I consulted over the last few days are what you might call 'circumspect'. That's putting it mildly. Especially John Morgan and Gang Tian. None of the extensive verification they've done in the last two years has called into question your proof or its completeness. Many of your peers think its a bluff by Yau to get in on the glory a few weeks ahead of the ICM in Madrid. The really suspicious one's mutter about the Clay Foundation's million-dollar prize. But that would be insulting Yau, I think. We all know how he'd always dreamed of solving the Conjecture."

"Of course. What mathematician hasn't? It's like asking the Knights of the Round Table if they've ever dreamt of finding the Grail. Richard Hamilton thought about it day and night. Worse yet, he thought he had it. I'd bet that even Gang Tian, a pure soul if ever there was one, has fantasized about it from time to time. Honestly, as a motive for a crime, you must agree it is weak."

"I don't understand you at all. It's as though this whole mess doesn't affect you at all."

"Come on, John. Try harder. I published my work almost three years ago. Time and tide, you know. The first flush of emotion has cooled. At the beginning, I was very concerned about what my colleagues thought. When I was asked to present my results at the creme-de-la-creme of American Universities, I said "Yes, why not?" You see where that got me? Three years later and the doubts are still rolling in. I am cured of that particular neurosis. I have very low expectations of mathematicians. Almost all of them are conformists. They are more or less honest, but they tolerate those who are not honest."

"Some say your indifference goes back further. Is it true, for instance, that you never answered questions from John Morgan and Gang Tian?

"That's not true," blurted Grigori. "I answered every one of their messages."

"But you didn't validate their work..."

"That would have been totally meaningless. The point of their work was to validate *mine*. Why on Earth would anyone want me to validate the validation of my own results?"

"How about to confirm that their interpretation was correct?"

"That's absurd. Imagine that Picasso, after finishing *Guernica,* receives a 400-page document written by eminent American art critics in view to explaining the meaning of the picture and announcing to the world that the canvas is a world-class masterpiece. Do you think Picasso would provide commentary on the book? Would anyone expect him to? I'll say it again. It makes no sense. My work was done. I published it. It's not mine anymore. I spent weeks explaining my reasoning in minute detail to hundreds of students and researchers in the US. I answered every serious question anyone asked me. Like it or not, my part is over."

"Some people may have taken your indifference for contempt."

"Some people. Certain parties. Who? Mathematicians in suits and ties who get together to hand out prizes? Them? I confess, I do despise them sometimes. But I have nothing but respect for Gang Tian. I'm very fond of him. We had some wonderful times together when we were both post-docs in New York during the '90s. We used to have intense discussions about our work. I remember one of the times we went to Princeton together to hear a lecture at the Institute. We talked for hours. I can recall the conversation like it was yesterday. It's a precious memory. And Tian is a remarkable mathematician, by the way. Why would I want to humiliate him?"

Gang and Morgan had sacrificed more than two years of their lives to unravelling Perelman's work. They had verified each hypothesis, lemma and intermediate equation. They slogged through the logical chain leading to his results. As their investigation moved forward, they became convinced that Perelman really had solved the most emblematic of the Millennium problems. A long and thankless two years it was. But it had been crucial that they eliminate all doubt, lift the clouds of suspicion, nip protests in the bud and stifle any jealousy.

It had all started a few years earlier, on November 11, 2002. That day, Grigori Perelman, who had not left his native Saint Petersburg for seven years—in fact, he'd practically been invisible—uploaded thirty-nine pages of text to a free online platform reserved for academic researchers. Following this first contribution, which was short but dense, Perelman published a second article a few weeks later. The first of these was titled "The Entropy Formula for the Ricci Flow and Its Geometric Applications." The second was called "Ricci Flow with Surgery on Three-Manifolds." Oddly enough, there was absolutely no explicit mention of the Poincaré

Conjecture in either. Had Perelman sought to shroud his research in a cloak of mystery? In point of fact, the significant developments he elaborated in the two articles went well beyond this particular problem. In them, he proved a more general case, known as the Thurston Conjecture. The Poincaré Conjecture, which had resisted the ongoing assaults of topology's most brilliant specialists for a century thus found itself relegated to the status of a particular case of a theorem.

As much or more than the content itself, it was Perelman's method that shocked the academic community and caused the initial kickback. The arXiv platform where Perelman presented his results is an archiving site where researchers—biologists, mathematicians, physicists and astrophysicists mostly—are wont to share their research at an intermediary stage, before it is submitted to peer reviewed journals. Distributing a completed article without simultaneously sending it to an academic periodical for publication was hardly common practice. Publication is the cornerstone of validation for scientific research, an obstacle course considered irreplaceable by many. Indeed, the Clay Foundation had made publication in a reputable journal a prerequisite for receiving the million-dollar prize set aside for solving any of the "Millennium Problems."

In order to be accepted by a journal, articles are subjected to an initial review assessing the rigor and method of their research. After that, they must be signed off on by a committee of independent specialists. This generally takes several months, sometimes years. Perelman had bypassed these steps, daringly illustrating his impudent disregard for rules. Only the truth mattered. His demonstration was accurate. He would not stoop to asking for validation from shadowy committees of readers. He knew that in doing so he would tick off most of his colleagues, but he wasn't much fussed about petty scandals.

Morgan and Tian found the process especially rough going. It turned out that reading a Perelman proof was almost as challenging as taking up the topic with him in person. To be fair, his sentences when speaking were clear, grammatically correct and sometimes even formally rather beautiful. Nonetheless they tended to betray a highly personal way of thinking. You might seize their literal content but their meaning would escape you. In writing, even when it came to expressing a mathematical reasoning, this gap persisted. The problem for the reader, however competent and alert, was not so much the language itself, which Perelman had come to master with time. It was the use he made of language. In other words, the issue was his mental process. In developing his argument, Perelman liked to recount the steps that led him to the solution, like a storyteller slowly peels back layers to reveal the secret their tale is built around. The journey from A to B involved making any number of pointless detours as well as taking great leaps. The latter would then require days of work to build bridges that were easier to cross. His reader would be compelled to trudge in Grigori's footsteps, falling down and scrambling up again. He or she must trust in the guide, clinging to the hope—one might say faith—that the road would eventually arrive at its scheduled destination.

Not content with the oddly sentimental answer Perelman had given, Ball pushed on with his argument. He sensed he had touched a weak spot.

"Alright. Let's say you didn't feel a response was needed to the complimentary exegesis of your work provided by Morgan and Tian, two mathematicians you know and like. There is, consequently, no reason you should give any more weight to the insidious critique by Cao and Zhu, two academics you don't even know. Have I summed it up, more or less?"

"Perfectly."

"What if you were more subtle, Grigori? If you accept the Fields Medal, wouldn't that be the most elegant way of paying homage to Morgan and Tian, as well as Kleiner and Lott and everyone else who expressed amazement at your discoveries? Everyone who spent days and nights decoding your flashes, never doubting their truth? And by the same token, it would brush aside with the indifference they deserve all those who, out of jealousy or otherwise, made a virtue of finding imaginary faults?"

"Leave me alone, John. You're not in a church, preaching. In a few months, you'll find this whole drama obscene and insignificant. Gang Tian will, I'm sure, be enraptured with some new, more fascinating topic. And as for Cao and Zhu..."

Perelman suddenly stiffened and clapped his right hand to his ear. His face was a horrible grimace of pain. His eyes were closed and his lips so tight he looked to bite right through them. His head tilted, resting heavily on the supporting hand. The whole ordeal lasted only a few seconds, as though he alone had been exposed to a piercing sound.

"Are you all right?" John asked, concerned. While aware that some people with autism suffer from hyperacusis, he couldn't help but suspect a ruse on the part of his adversary, a way of terminating the uncomfortable conversation.

"It's that racket. Can you hear it? It's not just a noise in your ears, it goes right through you. A terrible roar that fills you up and gets into every corner of your soul. One doesn't like it, but there you are, stuck in it, so you have to try and move around in it. So hard, it's so sticky. A huge empty noise that stifles everything. It gets in everywhere, bouncing around, echoing endlessly in signs that get weaker and weaker, drained of meaning. And the worst is when you realize your own voice is part of that racket, contributing to this drone, this death song, and even liking it. We all want others to recognize our own tiny voice amidst the uproar, but it's hopeless. You end up not even hearing yourself. It gets dissolved. If only it meant having your speech join a powerful flux. Something more, something transcendent. But no, it's just about howling louder than the next wolf, yowling, sneering, cruel cackling laughter, sardonic and depraved. It's getting ahead at any price, never mind the message, never mind that someone else said the same thing better, or first. It's the reign of plagiarism and stupidity. That's what pushes me away from the world. Can you understand?"

"I do understand, although I admit I don't quite experience the racket in your physical terms. Sometimes I dream of being like poets who recite their works in secret gatherings, or monks in the library of some abbey—I imagine finding a measure of comfort in hushed rooms where the learned confer."

"That's a sorry illusion, and you know it. You'd see exactly the same posturing, the same jockeying for position, the petty jealousies, the leering faces of idea-stealers. And, probably, the highest concentration of self-satisfaction that humanity has ever known."

As their conversation moved forward, John Ball saw, little by little the full depth of what Perelman would not tell him, could not tell him. He glimpsed the extended monologues cycling through the Russian's brain until they were worn to shreds. Things he was incapable of putting into words. He felt there was no point in trying to understand Perelman all of a piece. The most long-winded of his utterances would never be more than the tip of some iceberg.

It's at this moment that he had the idea of using his own mind as a receptacle. Like a chemist uses a test tube for an experiment. He could simply imagine the Russian mathematician's thoughts, immerse his mind in Perelman's. That he could do. All he needed were some clues, some weigh points. He began asking idle questions, inoffensive queries, hoping to find a hidden door, a passkey. He was looking for footprints, a trail. On the basis of these few details, meagre foundations, he began to devise his theory. It was a lot like the partial differential equations he mastered so well. Mathematical enigmas you tried to resolve starting only from their effects, from a few manifestations, and their derivatives at particular points in space.

John Ball embarked on solving the Perelman equation.

The day continued on lightly enough. They walked. They talked. No sparring, no debates. They ate a modest lunch at a *stolovaya*, one of those typical cafeterias left over from the Soviet era. Not once did John mention the Fields Medal, the Poincaré Conjecture or Chinese mathematicians. He held off on the King of Spain and the Clay Foundation's million dollars as well.

"Let's meet tomorrow in front of the Steklov," said Perelman when he considered it time to leave his companion.

John Ball suggested that Grigori join him for dinner. He had nothing planned. He hadn't gotten in touch with any of his Russian friends in order to focus entirely on his mission and to avoid arousing suspicion as to why he was there. What's more, the hotel's restaurant was quite acceptable.

"Perhaps we could just have a local dish and a bit of vodka," suggested Ball, not to encroach on his time.

"Thanks, really. But my mother is expecting me," the Russian replied politely.

True, his mother was waiting, she had dinner ready. As it was every night, the table would be laid when he came home. Two white plates, facing each other on a freshly ironed tablecloth of white lace. From the kitchen, the smell of hot borscht would waft out, filling the room. Ball didn't press him. Grigori wished to return to his family nest. Was nest the right word? It was more like a cell. A cell reduced to its core, to its inseparable component. Everything else had been evacuated: the world at large, and the world around, social obligations, neighbors, the community of mathematicians—

or what was left of it—even the other members of the family. The father had left. The Oedipal son was free of rivals. The sister had joined the father in his exile. Or rather, his "return" to the promised land.

"Exile is an ambiguous concept," thought Ball to himself. "A state of being rather than a geographical reality, a rule rather than an exception. Where do we come from? What land do we belong to? Which of the two, father or son, is the exile? Which is the victim, the mother or the son?" The mathematician lost himself in speculation. Exiled or not, victims or not, there they were, in a small apartment in Saint Petersburg, an inextricable couple perpetually alone—a mother living only through her progeny/prodigy and a genius who sees the shape of the universe and obediently eats his soup each night in the silence of his mother's apartment.

June 11, 2006, evening

It was eight-thirty in the evening. Daylight persisted, undaunted, its light pouring out from some seemingly unquenchable spring. The two men had walked all day. Too much. Too fast. John Ball was exhausted. He no longer had the strength of his youth, when he could play several tennis matches back to back on the lawn of his college at Cambridge. These days his legs were weaker, his arms had lost their power. His knees gave him trouble and his heart rate spiked at the slightest effort. The Russian mathematician, by comparison, had seemed to him a force of nature. Their ramble had underscored the almost two decades that separated the two. Nonetheless, Ball had made the best of it, keeping the pace set by his colleague without complaint. Back in his hotel room, though, he had collapsed on the bed like a wild animal struck by lightening. This respite, however, did not last long.

A few minutes later, the telephone in his bedroom went off. It rang once, then twice, three times. At the third ring, John Ball made up his mind to answer. It couldn't be his wife, she would have called his mobile. He checked at a glance. No missed calls. Was it Perelman? Did he have something important, something urgent to communicate? Something he'd forgotten, a regret, a revelation?

"John Ball speaking."

The voice that answered him at the other end of the line was not one he recognized. This man spoke excellent English, tinged with a strong, typically Russian accent. From the first words he uttered, he spoke to Ball with an exaggerated deference too pompous to be natural.

"Good evening Professor Sir John Ball. My name is Sergei Rukshin. I would like to speak with you, if you have no objections to doing so. Would you be so kind as to meet me at the bar of your hotel?"

"I am very tired," answered Ball. "Can't it wait for tomorrow?"

"I'm afraid not, Professor, sir. I would like you discuss with you certain confidential matters regarding Grigori.

"All right, very well. I'll be downstairs in ten minutes."

Ball knew next to nothing about Sergei Rukshin. He had a vague notion that the name had come up once or twice in the biographical notes he'd gone over on the plane, but he hadn't paid it any mind.

Who was this man who had come and hunted him up at his hotel room? When he got to the bar, there was no mistake to be made. Only one individual was waiting. He stood, unmoving in front of the bar counter. An imposing figure. He wore a heavy coat of bronze-colored wool, a totally superfluous garment given the season. His hands were buried in his pockets. He had hollow cheeks covered in freckles, partially hidden by a light-colored beard, thick but neatly trimmed. His gaze moved methodically around the room, like a scanner registering the environment. He seemed anxious.

Ball approached him. The man shot out his hand hastily, staring at him fixedly.

"I am most honored to make your acquaintance Professor."

"Likewise. Delighted. Shall we sit here?" asked Ball, indicating two comfortable mahogany armchairs upholstered in red velvet away from the main passage. Something to drink?"

"Yes, thank you. Vodka."

The man dropped into the ample seat without even removing his coat, breathing heavily. He seemed anxious to speak, like an ambassador who has journeyed hundreds of miles to deliver an urgent message. The kind of message that changes the course of history. He was waiting for a sign he might begin.

Sergei Rukshin was possibly the only person to have deeply plumbed the soul of Grigori Perelman. Exception made for his mother, of course. He was nineteen when he met Grigori for the first time. This was during the mid 1970s, that obscure period when the Soviet Union began, silently, to unravel. Sergei was finishing his dissertation in mathematics at the University of Leningrad. And, two afternoons a week, he coached a math club of Young Pioneers. At the time, he had been an uncouth and solitary young man, a hanger-on in a fast crowd, getting in trouble more than was good for him. But he was, above all, a young man frustrated that he lacked the intellectual abilities to rise as high as his tremendous ambition urged.

"So, you wanted to talk to me about Grigori Perelman, you said?" Ball finally asked.

"Well yes, quite. I am his math teacher."

"You're his math teacher. What are you talking about? Grigori Perelman solved the Poincaré Conjecture. I find it hard to believe he needs a math teacher."

"I was his first math teacher, if you prefer. But I would like to believe that Grigori still considers me his teacher. One who receives instruction from a master remains forever his student, don't you think? Here in Russia, the son never becomes the father. Perhaps things are different where you come from, in England, Professor."

Ball struggled to keep his temper. He found this man exasperating. He had turned up without warning, jerked John from the sleep he desperately needed after his strenuous day, and now he was lecturing him with academic parables? What cheek. Arrogance, he thought.

"Very good. Let's hear what you have to say. I'm afraid I've forgotten your name, mister...?"

"I am Sergei Rukshin."

"What do you want to tell me, Mr. Rukshin?"

"I've come to ask you to go back home."

The words fell on him like a court sentence. The Englishman slumped in his chair. He remained silent a time, staring at his nighttime visitor in shock, waiting for something more. An explanation. An apology. Nothing further was offered.

"That's it?"

"Yes. Well, I wanted to convince you, or at least try to convince you, to stop pestering Grigori, you see. Nothing will come of it. He won't go to Madrid, and you know it. This confrontation you're inflicting on him isn't doing him any good, you must see that. I mean, you do understand, don't you?"

Rukshin had abandoned his peremptory tone and was becoming more and more agitated. He had sworn he would be brief, straightforward and intransigent, but John Ball's short, contemptuous reply had tumbled him back into the clammy arms of the anxiety he hated. He was a child again, stuck in a grim Leningrad suburb, getting mixed up in low-grade trafficking and other unsavory machinations, quick to use his fists over trifles. Of course, he'd succeeded in channeling this violence, he hadn't hit anyone in thirty years, but that inner tension never left him. He must regain control of the conversation. "Back to basics," he told himself. "set out the hypotheses and formulate the problem."

"When Grisha, I mean Grigori, was brought to me, he had just turned ten. He was a scrawny boy. Socially inept and boring. I had been coaching the Young Pioneers club for two years. Not to blow my own horn, but I had begun to achieve real results with the youngsters. I took him into the group because he came recommended by a professor at Herzen University. He got a leg up, you might say. For my part, I was not looking for quantity, but quality. My group was already established, and I didn't like taking on new students after the year had begun. His mother came to see me one evening at the Palace of Young Pioneers. She was a young woman with dark hair. A little chubby, but well put together and very persuasive. Very sure of herself. Grigori stood behind her. I don't think he spoke a single word the whole time. He rocked back and forth, chewing on a pencil, looking up at her with something like veneration. He has always been obsessed with his mother, but if you had seen her that night, her determination, you would understand why."

"Go on," John Ball encouraged him, after a moment of silence had elapsed.

"Grigori became my favorite student. Teacher's pet, as they say in grammar school. Don't get me wrong. I never favored him in training sessions. I'd call on him last, because he always had the right answer. It was to give the others a chance. I wanted to hear each one of them express their chain of thought. The other boys assumed I did so because Grigori seemed so fragile, so they put up with it, but it wasn't a very convincing explanation. I have no time for the weak. Grigori was not weak. Granted, he had trouble expressing himself. It was as though words would jam up in his mouth and tumble out all mixed up in uncontrolled bursts. He also behaved oddly when he was thinking. He would twist around in his chair, swinging his head and lifting his chin. Tapping on the table. He looked like he was possessed. But none of that was weakness. The most important thing for me was that he was still malleable. I needed material to work with that was both strong and supple for my methods to be effective. I wanted to prove that I was the best mathematics teacher in the world. A confirmed genius would have been no use to me. A weak vessel even less.

"Wouldn't the best evidence of this be for your student Grigori Perelman to receive the Fields Medal? Or don't you think so?"

Ball regretted his words almost as soon as they had left his mouth. "What an idiot," he berated himself. "That was subtle, not." Unsurprisingly, the Russian responded angrily.

"Your flattery is not welcome, Professor Ball. My students have achieved more than seventy medals at the Math Olympiads, forty of them gold. The proof of my pedagogical abilities was delivered long ago. When a proof is complete, there is no need to add pages of superfluous commentary."

His rage bubbled up again. Sergei Rukshin's whole body struggled with his demons. His nerves were on fire. "This conversation is going nowhere," he thought. Now or never. Must regroup. He shook himself and tried to pick up where he had left off.

"I didn't immediately spot his talent. Many of his classmates at the club showed more natural inclination for mathematics. I remember Boris Sudakov and Alexander Golovanov especially. They had all the hallmarks of future genius. They were constantly honing their reasoning skills, spoiling for a fight. For them, math problems were like ritual initiations, virtual battlegrounds where the two boys would lock horns in a show of male dominance. From this point of view, a math club and a sports club have a lot in common.

Grigori was different. Most of the time he was silent. Contemplative, is maybe the word. He was content to watch his comrades engage in intellectual jousting. Where the other boys used mathematics as a pretext for building social bonds, Grigori was busy building a whole other world, entirely inside himself. It finally dawned on me that, instead of talking to other *people* about mathematics, he talked *to* mathematics."

"And you tried to communicate with him?"

"I was testing my teaching method."

"But Grigori was more than just a student to you, wasn't he? A spiritual son?"

"I had found my ideal disciple. I was fascinated by the way he reasoned. His behavior might seem eccentric, but you had to look at his mind the way you would approach a mathematical problem. Considered this way, Perelman was a puzzle. There would be a solution. He operated like a complex system. The more energy I devoted to him, the more we became symbiotic, and an unbelievable network of solutions opened up to me."

Rukshin stopped talking, calm once again and deeply immersed in his memories.

"Alright then," said Ball. "So, you, more than anyone else, have explored the depths of Grigori Perelman's soul. You are partially responsible for shaping his intelligence, refining his mechanics. You have contributed to making him one of the world's greatest mathematicians, and the pride you derive from that gives meaning to your existence. And you came to ask me to stop pestering him, is that right?"

"Yes. I knew you'd understand."

"But, why?"

Sergei Rukshin's face became a study in suffering and sadness. His eyes filled with tears and his lip trembled. For just a second there, he had believed Ball had actually heard his message. It was a horrible jolt to realize this wasn't the case at all. From there, his speech parted company with reason. His sentences rambled, nebulous and enigmatic. He asked question after question, but answered none; doors that opened only onto other doorways. His unsavory rhetoric teetered on the edge of conspiracy theory.

"What are you thinking? Do you really believe you know Grisha's whole story? Have you grasped the scope of his message? He has spent his life tracking down holes in our world. Do you have any idea what that means? Do you truly imagine that it's all only about math? Don't be naive. The world has changed, Professor Ball. This city used to be called Leningrad, remember? There were holes everywhere you looked in our society. Grisha disappeared for *seven years*. I know it didn't take him seven years to solve the Conjecture. It was a period of political unrest, of blind violence. It was social disaster. You know nothing of that. You were nice and safe in your decadent West, believing the end of history was within reach. Grisha is part of something enormous, a movement so great you cannot even perceive its echo. He has achieved his dream. Have you studied Kaballah? It contains every question there is. Grisha has completed a mystical quest. He knows the shape of the universe. Can you wrap your mind around that? Forget the Ricci flow, forget Hamilton. Flotsam, mere technicalities. I'm talking to you about intimate knowledge of the soul of the universe. Stay out of it, Professor Ball."

A few minutes went by. It might have been an hour. Perhaps more. The bar at the Hotel Kempinski had emptied out. Sergei had gone. John Ball sat alone with his glass of vodka. His head was killing him. He shouldn't have drunk so much. How much exactly? He couldn't remember. They had reordered several times, of that he was certain. An empty bottle lay like a corpse on the table. "*A quarter of all Russian men die before the age of 55,*" he had read in a magazine somewhere. A passion for vodka was probably a significant contributor to that macabre statistic. The visit from that man, Sergei Rukshin had left him feeling uneasy, though his shock had subsided. What was he after? Had he come on his own advice or bidden? If the latter, by whom? Perelman himself? Unlikely. His mother then? Underground groups with an interest of some sort in the work of the Russian mathematician? Spies? Kabbalists? The surfeit of alcohol had his head spinning. He was no longer sure he had actually heard Rukshin telling him about Kabbalists. Perhaps they'd already both been dead drunk by that point in their conversation.

Be reasonable, Ball kept telling himself. Rukshin wanted to protect Grigori, protect him from needless suffering. That's all. After all, he knew the man well enough to understand his weaknesses, the human side of the genius you might say. He had been much more than Grigori's math coach. He had replaced the boy's father in some ways. Ball suddenly felt silly for having treated his visitor so harshly.

He glanced at his watch. Eleven thirty. He considered going back out, into the joyful streets of the city as it celebrated Baltic springtime. The pain in his head would not let up. It was like a gong beat time on his temples. He kept telling himself to be reasonable, but those references to manipulation and conspiracy ate at him. Were they a product of Rukshin's paranoia or his own delirium? How could he find out? He needed some clarity within. John Ball went back up to his room, swallowed one of the migraine pills he always kept in his toiletries and threw himself into the files he had brought along. These consisted of a few dozen pages of notes written up by the secretariat of the World Mathematics Society on the life and work of Grigori Perelman. He went over them looking for holes. Those famous holes. Where were they hiding? What did they mean? How had these details escaped him?

Going over his notes, which he did with care, everything had seemed on track in the life of Grigori Perelman until the mid-1990s. He was on the "usual" trajectory of a promising young academic. At the time, these great minds, wherever they hailed from originally, all made an obligatory stop at the campus of some American university. "Not much has changed," thought Ball in passing. Grigori made a point of conscientiously completing this crucial step on the path to success. He didn't even complain. He started at SUNY Stony Brook, not far from New York City, then continued his work at a UC Berkley lab in California. He met other mathematicians from all over the world. Most of all, he met great professors, giants in their fields. Richard Hamilton, for one, whose work on the Ricci flow he admired. He had already solved several major problems in geometry and was headed for a standard issue career as an academic. Job offers rolled in. East Coast, West Coast, he could take his pick.

That's where the break came. A huge hole had begun to take shape in Perelman's biography. One by one, he rejected every offer made to him. Brutally, over trivialities. When asked for a CV, he refused to comply. When they indulged his every whim, he said it was too late. After two years spent away from his hometown, he returned to Saint Petersburg and moved back in with his mother, who had lived alone since his father and sister had left for Israel. From that moment on, he disappeared almost entirely from the realm of mathematics. In seven years, he did not publish a single article, make any trips outside Russia or attend one major conference. A gaping emptiness.

John Ball struggled to gather the scattered pieces of the puzzle. Like the scientist he could not help being, he parsed the available information. Why had the young Russian, who regularly sent a portion of his salary home to his mother, refused the golden handshake and red-carpet treatment rolled out by the most prestigious American universities? Was it arrogance? Was it merely, as he claimed, because he was unwilling to teach so much as a few hours a week? Did he want to devote himself full time, without any distractions, to what he had already glimpsed might be a major step forward? Did he know, even then, that he could prove the Poincaré Conjecture? Perhaps he understood that to do so he needed unbounded time, true silence and a familiar environment. And for that he needed to leave behind the ultracompetitive jungle of Ivy League campuses. Or had he been pulled back to the mother country by darker forces, as the mysterious Sergei Rukshin had seemed to suggest? But if so, what were they?

John Ball fell into sleep, a slumber shot with violent, fleeting dreams. Misty scenes flitted by, teeming with kabbalists certain that the resolution of Poincaré's conjecture was an essential key to unlocking the meaning of their sacred texts. Mafia gangs joined the throng, eager to turn the discovery into cash by way of the industrial-military complex. Incandescent politicians set out to heal social divisions with mathematical equations. He kept waking up, disoriented and sweating, even though his hotel room's A/C was set to 69 degrees.

His files were spread out all over the bed. Exhausted by the tug-o-war between consciousness and febrile visions, he was finding it harder and harder to distinguish between reality and his imagination. Had Grigori Perelman's first math teacher really paid him a visit the night before? He was finding it harder and harder to believe.

June 11, 2006, night

In the last hours of their walk around the historic center of Saint Petersburg, John Ball had begun to hear, more and more distinctly, sentences that Grigori Perelman had not spoken aloud. These were not what you would, properly speaking, call hallucinations. Nor were they the desperate fantasies of a man hoping against hope for a miracle.

He really heard.

Without question, it was Grigori Perelman's thoughts that were expressed. And in some extraordinary way, John Ball had accessed them. It was a bit like a simultaneous translation. He would close his eyes for a second or two and suddenly feel like a technician had pressed play on a scratchy recording in his ears. He was certain he had understood something—he'd brushed up against a mystery only faith could explain. Ball normally went in for neither mysticism nor divination. You would never catch him subbing in for Moses before the burning bush. No more than he would imagine himself the Oracle at Delphi! What had happened was this. He had gradually become convinced that in order to manage the contradictions of Perelman's mind, he would have to immerse himself in the latter's thoughts, to drown in them if need be. The day's conversations, with all their detours and pinnacles, their silences and misunderstandings, had ultimately woven an intelligible whole. The key was to have enough courage to let his imagination do the work, to let his intelligence do the work, as Perelman kept suggesting. That meant using it to fill in holes, repair uneven spots, iron out creases and erase dangerous cracks so as not to be swallowed up, body and soul. It meant being ready to step into Grigori's space, a mental space that must—one way or another—be homeomorphic to a human brain.

So, when John Ball found himself awake in the middle of the night, tired of struggling with his nightmares, he naturally started listening again. Settled comfortably into an armchair in the corner of his room, he let his eyelids fall like curtains. He took three deep breaths, breathing in as far as possible, expanding his chest and feeling his body open like a flower, then loudly emptying his lungs to expel every last molecule of carbon dioxide. This was his standard procedure for beginning his meditation sessions. His mind became blank. He was ready to welcome someone else's interior world.

That's when Grigori's voice piped up inside him.

When I was little—Mamma used to tell me without ever explaining why that one is a child until the age of thirteen—I used to like winning prizes. I was proud to climb onstage. I'd look out into the sea of faces for Mamma as I shook the rough hands of the local brass. They were always aged gentlemen in tattered military dress, peppered with medals whose gilding was fading suspiciously. Almost certainly received for exploits far less glorious than my own, I used to tell myself. Naturally, I already despised those who gave me these prizes, but my childish self-importance was enough to carry me through despite the mediocrity of my temporary masters. I did them the honor of appearing, that's all. It made Mamma happy, which was the main thing for me. She would smile. Always dignified, always off to one side. She never sat up front. Even when competitions were held far away, like Moscow, or in other cities around the USSR even further away, she was always there. Cold and fatigue were nothing to her. She would leave my father and sister for hours, even days. And there she would be, in the second or third row, braced on the armrests to look out over the epaulettes of the army types seated in front of her. She would sit there the whole time, with her chin up and eyes wide as though witnessing a miracle.

Mamma won't go to Madrid. Even if I asked her to. Even if I begged her. She's too old now. Her legs are swollen and covered in blue veins. Airplanes make her ill. Besides, there would be too many people this time. Crowds make her nervous. Who would look after her? She might not even have her own reserved seat in the second or third row. And anyway, it's been ages since she sat in a hall waiting for me to receive a prize. I'm not a child anymore.

She must have forgotten. Her memory is still sharp for someone her age, but I'm sure the details have faded. I, on the other hand, can recall every ceremony, from the shape of the stage to the height of each step. From the color of the chairs in the room to the puffy faces of the motheaten national heroes lined up like bowling pins in the front row. I don't forget much, on the whole. "Grigori is too focused on details," Mamma used to say when I was little.

Meanwhile, I discovered the shape of the universe. That's not a detail.

I remember the end-of-year awards ceremony for Secondary School 239, the magnet school for Leningrad. I can also recall the more modest mathematics club prizes, little silver or gilded cups, probably bought at basement prices at some flea market by our coach. And, of course, I remember the actual gold medal from the Math Olympiad, when I was sixteen. Every time, I'd experience the exact same frustration. When I'd climb down from the podium, I'd turn around and look at the ignorant hierarchs parading around the stage. I realized early that awards ceremonies exist to show off the givers, not the recipients of prizes.

It all started well enough. I liked the place I used to go three times a week. At first, Mamma used to come with me—the others used to smirk, but I wasn't ashamed. Why should I be ashamed? It was called a math club—the way there were basketball clubs or track and field clubs. And believe me, there was a real similarity. The Soviet conception of intellectual contests at the time was not very different from the sporting challenges of Ancient Greece. In our society, with its perpetual revolution, the intellectual, athletic and political dimensions were all twisted into one. Remember the international uproars over the Chess world championships in the early seventies? Spassky vs Fisher? No laughing matter. The honor of the nation was at stake. More than that, the supremacy of our model society, or semblance thereof, hung in the balance.

It was the highest plane of the Cold War. The two blocs played out in fictional battlegrounds the war that could not be fought in the theater of reality. And mathematicians had a seat at the high table in the regime's pantheon. The Soviet Union trained the best mathematicians in the world, there could be absolutely no doubt of this. So, to prepare us algebra and geometry-wielding child-soldiers, they trained us like high-performance athletes. Schools scouted the most promising students extremely early, as young or nine or ten, like gymnasts. In the one case they used IQ tests, in the other bone measurements and muscular development. Then, of course, we'd be enrolled in those famous clubs, and the real training began.

Physical activity played a major part in the curriculum. On Sundays, the whole team would get together in the countryside or forest. A brilliant mind cannot blossom in a frail body, our teachers would repeat, time and again. We would scramble dozens of miles in the woods around Saint Petersburg, until winter and snow made it impossible. We threw ourselves vigorously into developing our adolescent bodies. We were encouraged to value solidarity and foster an esprit de corps. I was awkward and scrawny. I'd trip on tree roots and come home with bruises and scratches all over my legs. But I enjoyed it. It was exhilarating. When I was selected for the Russian team in the Math Olympiads we went east. Way east, far from our families. Not Siberia, of course, but we were sufficiently isolated to think of nothing but the tremendous mission the Soviet Union had entrusted us with. Fight the good fight. Prevail. And receive those lovely medals from a bunch of conceited leaders, peacocks who can hardly count. That's why I won't ask Mamma to go to Madrid.

A King, you say? So what? Why should this farce be more acceptable with a king, even if he were the direct descendant of the monarchs who reigned over Castile and Aragon? Do you think vanity is inversely proportional to prestige of office or quality of pedigree? No. Mamma won't come, and I will not come get the Fields Medal. I feel sick just thinking about it. I can imagine the stage, draped in red velvet, set up in the ball room of some Spanish Renaissance palace in Madrid, the same building where the Inquisition could have been condemning Jews to the stake. They haven't renounced yet—they're still determined to force a conversion out of me. But I resist, like a marrano. *I can see myself treading a garnet carpet, decorated with the Bourbon coat of arms. Around my neck dangles a heavy medal embossed with a portrait of Archimedes and quotation from the poet Manilius*: 'Surpass your own mind and seize the universe.' *Around the rim, my name is inscribed in Cyrillic letters. How thoughtful. I turn around, and there are the same ignorant hierarchs in full regalia. Their chests tinkle with the same undeserved medals. I can see them parading on stage: princes and counts, princesses, and marquesses, with a King in the middle, substituting nicely for the Secretary of the Presidium of the Supreme Soviet. I feel humiliated. My place is on the stage to begin with. I should be the one looking down on them, watching them descend into the crowd to salute me with deep humility when they turn around. I could be a king, but this king of Spain could never be a mathematician. What does he know about Alexandrov Spaces? No, I won't go.*

The blackout curtains were drawn tight, and only the slightest artificial light illuminated the room. It was barely possible to identify the furnishings. By closing his eyes and concentrating on his breathing, focusing on the air entering and leaving his lungs, Ball was able to direct himself entirely inward. This way, he could clearly visualize Perelman's face, his almond eyes with their blue iris, his forehead crossed with heavy horizontal lines. Most of all, he could listen to him. He had broadened his mind enough to incorporate the noises around. At this point, even the maddening growl of the air conditioning failed to bother him.

He could distinctly hear Perelman. It was a different Perelman. No longer was he a Moses "of slow speech and slow of tongue." The stiffness and tics of autism made way for a smooth flow of discourse unhampered by the slight stutter that, in the real world, impeded his thoughts. Ball kept his concentration steady. Every time a parasitic thought cropped up he did everything he could to avoid letting his attention wander. For instance, when he hoped that a desire to wear the laurel wreath might be taking root somewhere in Perelman's mind. He tried to let it go its own way naturally. Each time, he brought his focus back to his breathing, and Perelman's voice rang out again. Ball felt no need to respond to this monologue, no inclination to confrontation. It was enough to be at the receiving end, flooded with the Russian mathematician's thoughts and welcoming them.

One day I was at the suite of some grand hotel in Paris with gilding all over the walls and moldings on the ceiling. There were two armchairs upholstered in creamy fabric embroidered in red silk and arms made of white wood. Scattered around, there was a rather harmonious assortment of furnishings from various periods.

I recall a Louis XIV dresser with a huge mirror, an Empire chair. Facing the window was a tapestry from the Gobelins workshop with a hunting scene. There were modern sofas in the middle of the room, and that's where we sat—some journalist asked me to explain what I'd discovered. "In a few words," he specified.

"So, what exactly is this Poincaré Conjecture," he added, "I mean, for someone who knows nothing about math, like me for one, and the vast majority of our readers? Could you summarize what its about, I mean, just the essentials, the concept? I'd be most interested. As you know, Poincaré is like a piece of France's genius. He's a beacon of sorts, which you have lit anew," he went on. "Today, people have no idea, they confused Henri with his cousin Raymond. It's so sad! As though political power was anything next to the greatness of science."

My silence encouraged him to continue his monologue. It occurred to me that he could just as well write his article without my input. Maybe his article would even be better if I didn't answer his questions, assuming he had a modicum of talent, of course.

"I'm afraid I can't explain it to you. The Poincaré Conjecture is much too simple an idea to be dissected in a few words." That's how I answered him. Naturally, he took the jest as me being haughty. I saw his eyebrows bow together, and his bony little body stiffen. He lost his verve. He looked to be on the verge of tears— eyes brimming with a mixture of anger and sadness. He tried rephrasing his question but got nowhere. We exchanged a few superficial remarks in between sips of tea. Then he apologized and left.

A few weeks later, when I was back in Saint Petersburg, I received a letter containing a magazine article, along with the journalist's card, on which he had simply written "Cordially" in French. The article was titled "Is the Universe a Sphere?" The first page featured a photo of me. A three-quarters view that was not particularly sympathetic. There followed three pages of pseudo-scientific rubbish, delivered with a certain literary flair. The journalist must have consulted a few mathematicians from amongst his acquaintances, and made up the rest. I could hardly fault him for it. In concluding his piece, he was kind enough to quote the remark he had taken as a slap in the face, and added, "It is sometimes the simplest questions that require the most complicated reasoning to answer."

I ran across this yellowing photocopy in a big manilla envelope where my mother had stuffed a bunch of articles about me. I'm not a fan of relics, but in this particular case, it's lucky this scrap of paper got saved. Lucky for you, I mean, my dear colleague. As I said, the author was rather a good writer. Very sprightly, almost lyrical. The paragraph I found interesting was this one. Judge for yourself:

"Is the thing we see as a sphere really a sphere? You may look infinitely for holes in a space and not find any, but how can you be sure that you have truly covered this space in every direction and explored each and every cranny? What if being close to the hole were enough to change your direction and prevent you from confronting reality? To avoid catastrophe, you would wind up going round and round in the safe portion of space, staying away from its fissures, which is the best possible way to convince yourself they simply don't exist. On the surface of our planet, a human thirst for adventure has saved us from this ignorance. Let's hear it for Magellan, Peary, Amundsen, Livingstone and Cousteau! For a long time now, we have known there is no valley, however steep its sides, from which it is impossible to climb, no deep ocean trench but that has a bottom on which to settle. Every mountain has a peak, from which to descend, assuming the weather cooperates. With all due respect to Dante, the gates of Hell are not to be found on Earth. Our planet is a surface without holes. A sphere, or close enough. Were it made of clay, one might easily shape it into a smooth and perfect ball. But what of the universe? When we add a new dimension to our space, what happens to our certainty? Is our Universe also a sphere? Naturally, no one can look at the shape of the universe, since for that one would have to be outside it. While we have left our planet and captured its rotund glory in the magnificent pictures taken by Apollo 8, there is no chance of leaving the all-containing universe. Does this prevent us from imagining the shape of this whole? Of course not. If our Universe is a sphere, it is a dimension-three sphere. Care to imagine what that looks like? Imagine for a moment that you are walking on a dimension-two sphere (the Earth's surface for instance), but at any time during your stroll, you might 'detach' yourself from the surface and find yourself on the surface of a different dimension-two sphere (another planet). You would then be at liberty to continue your trip on this new surface, or leave it at any moment to return to the original spherical surface. Such a ramble might last indefinitely—there are no holes in such a space."

Not bad for a philistine, don't you think? Unfortunately, like most of the people around us, journalists refuse to accept complexity and he was no exception. He opted for the half-full glass. An optimistic vision of the world he had glimpsed as he peered between the lines of my silence. "The world is definitely smooth," he thought. "You have only to go about the world unremittingly for this to become obvious."

But the alternative—the other side of the coin, I'd like to say— deserves some consideration. In this reality, the world is smooth only for he who is constantly repairing its cracks. Perfection is no longer a given waiting to be discovered, but a perpetual struggle. Let's be honest. Our environment is by no means inherently friendly. Anywhere you go, you might suddenly tumble into an infinite fissure or get lost in a dark tunnel without a light at its end. We are sometimes lulled into believing in a reassuring continuity, but it's a trick. The more the world appears accessible, the more full of traps it is. When it most invites our trust, that's when we must be wary of its pitfalls. To avoid them, we need strategies and schemes, but most of all, we need rigor and method. We must devise strategies so complex that the world itself won't see them coming. That is the only way to get back on top. I'm not talking about hiking or mountaineering here. The most gaping holes are the ones tearing at the fabric of our societies, ripping apart our countries, our cities, our families. Ultimately, it is this vast problem that I have spent ten years trying to solve. I'm not the only one trying to heal the imperfections around us, you know. I have lots of friends all over the world—Saint Petersburg, Moscow, the US, Paris. Like me, they're tirelessly looking for better roads, tested pathways that can avoid these artefacts. They are professors, teachers, social workers... some are doctors. Others are psychologists, obstinately laboring at the bedsides of tattered souls. Some are even street performers, musicians or poets. What they do each and every day is what I call social topology. The fractures they seek out are different, but the method for sealing them is the same. It involves taking the time to identify pathways and their risks, anticipating and repairing discontinuities. Repairing, constantly repairing. It's more than a science, it's a state of mind, a philosophy. It means accepting the world as a hostile but predictable surface, a damaged surface, riddled with scars that must be healed to move forward. It means accepting complexity. How am I supposed to explain concepts like that in a few words?

At certain points John Ball's mind wandered. His own internal voice took over, flitting from one topic to another with wicked enjoyment. From minor administrative matters to tragically chronic family issues, it tapped his obsessive fears and the rare temptations to stray that he proudly held at bay. It raised the specter of publications he wasn't writing as fast as he'd like and of the dozens of trips he kept promising himself he would take and always put off for later. This mission seemed to be having much greater consequences, personal ones, than he wanted to admit.

In examining Perelman's intimate relationship to success and acclaim, he ran the risk of falling into a dangerous chasm of introspection. Was this about his own consecration? Was he really able to remove himself from this highly personal matter? Hadn't he come to Saint Petersburg with the sole aim of preventing his moment of glory—the Congress—from being tinged with shadow? What importance did he himself attach to this prestigious moment? Did that make him one of those hierarchs Perelman so despised? Wasn't it true that he'd accepted to serve as president of the International Mathematical Union only to secure an honor that his work, however brilliant, would never deliver?

His interior voice became a prosecutor. Grigori Perelman had become no more than a pretext prompting a cross-examination of his own conscience. John Ball focused again on his breathing; making an effort to recreate the interior peace he enjoyed so much. He opened his consciousness well beyond the hotel room he sat in, beyond the city around him. He was then ready to receive the Russian's next words, as though listening to the piercing chants of Buddhist monks.

Now, I have no way to say how important this next point is to me. I can't say either whether it partly explains the wandering path I've taken or the direction of my research. But the fact is that I am Jewish. My father told me so, one winter night. It was one of those special evenings he spent with me only. After dinner, Mamma and my sister would leave us alone in the living room and he would pull a book out of his briefcase and we would read it together. As I read aloud, his finger would follow the lines like a yad—that ritual instrument rabbis run along the parchment while reading the Torah, which I only discovered much later.

That day, my father had brought home a big book on the theory of relativity, which he must have borrowed from the library. It was a thick science textbook, clearly very serious, with a hard cover that was either pink or beige, I can't remember. Inside its pages were full of equations and schematics I couldn't understand yet. The first part of the book, which can't have been more than a dozen pages or so, was dedicated to the life of Albert Einstein. It told of his peaceful youth in Austria, how he met Elsa, his first wife, on a bench of the University in Vienna. There was his obsessive pursuit of his research and the birth of their first son, Hans. Then came their second son Eduard, a tragic figure whose life dead-ended in an asylum. And ultimately, how he fled to America to escape the Nazis. At the end of this first part, there were four pages of black and white pictures. Most of them showed Einstein near the end of his life. In some he was very serious, posing rigidly with a stern glare. In others he was sardonic, flashing a self-deprecating smile at the camera. They'd been taken on campus at Princeton, in cafés, on New York streets. The book's author, whose name I've forgotten, had sought to achieve the miracle of compressing the life of a genius in ten pages of text and four of pictures.

From the standpoint of my ignorant 8-year-old self, I found the tale fascinating, probably because I couldn't decipher any more of the book. Today, such an attempt seems absurd. If you want to talk about the life of a scientist, limit yourself to describing his discoveries. Anything else is pointless. What can it possibly matter to us to know about Einstein, other than his theory? What end is served by dusting off his pettiness, his beliefs, his compromises? Do his fears, failed relationships, his cowardice or his abysmal record as a father teach us anything? Nothing it is possible to write about the life of Albert Einstein provides any insight into his incredible summary of space and time.

When we had finished reading this summary biography, my father closed the book and announced that we too—he himself, Mamma, Elena and I—were Jewish. He spoke these words in his official tone, the didactic and thoughtful voice he used when giving me history lessons. I didn't know what it meant. Still today, I don't think I do, even though I now perfectly comprehend every subtlety of the equations that book on relativity was full of. In the Soviet society of the period, being Jewish meant precisely nothing. At most it was a pedigree to be suppressed, a suspended memory, a state of being that was almost invisible, inaudible, practically no different from anyone else, a cold and modern form of Marranism.

Over the weeks and months that followed my father's revelation, I looked for manifestations of this new status. I needed proof. Little by little I managed to identify certain practices of our daily life with our Jewishness. Once a week, my mother would light a candle in a corner of the kitchen. And there was the handful of books in Hebrew on the top shelves of the bookcase. To this category also I assigned the lack of bread for a week each spring and that strange day in the fall when my father would do absolutely nothing at all. These were just clues, signs, unnatural behaviors. I never asked any questions. If these seemingly inexplicable actions had some secret to tell, I had no doubt of my capacity to pierce it without help, as easily as I solved the puzzles my father set me. And if, on the contrary, the mystery was to remain whole, then it was better all around that silence continue to enshroud this absence of meaning.

A few years later, I finished my secondary studies at Saint Petersburg's most prestigious high school, an elite institution reserved for youth identified as intellectually gifted. My professor called in my mother to tell her that I had proved I had the capabilities necessary for acceptance at the University in the Mathematics department. But whatever joy that brought was short-lived. Abashedly, he added immediately that it was practically impossible for a Jew to attend. The number of places that could be claimed by Jews was extremely limited. He deeply objected to such restrictions, he said, but that's how things were. Totalitarianism gains a foothold in a society when things that are unacceptable are considered immutable by all and sundry. My professor did not want to get her hopes up, he insisted. We would have to wait for the verdict handed down by a jury—with no way of knowing who was on it—and hope my name appeared on the short list of those selected. Basically, it was a blind lottery, a spin of the wheel of fortune by the anonymous hands of the bureaucratic beast.

My mother had no fondness for games of chance. The possibility of failure annoyed her. Failing was not an option she was prepared to consider, ever. She insisted. My instructor, who was a competent teacher and a good man, yielded to her determination. While passive and fatalistic, he was honest, and he finally disclosed to my mother that he might have an alternative solution. Each year, the winners of the Math Olympiad were exempted from the treacherous selection process and automatically granted their University enrollment papers.

My mother told me nothing about this meeting. I found out many years later. Anyway, I competed in the Olympiad. I knew nothing of the stakes, but I won. And just like that, I was no longer a Jew to be counted and herded like cattle. I'd become a Soviet hero. If my mother had told me the truth, if I'd known that my future hung in the balance, I might not have won the medal. Perhaps I might even have lost on purpose. But she didn't want me to feel inferior or different. Most of all, she didn't want me to feel Jewish. It was her form of resistance, of not bowing her head, but standing tall in the face of a system that wanted to see her on her knees—her way of showing strength and dignity. That's how I came to start at the University without knowing I didn't quite belong.

Come to think of it, the fact that I was born Jewish is of no importance. No more than was important for Albert Einstein, Niels Bohr and Robert Oppenheimer. Don't get me wrong, I'm not comparing myself to Einstein or Bohr—they were geniuses who radically transformed the way we see the world. I've done nothing more than confirm the brilliant intuition of a French mathematician from over a century ago. That we should all four happen to be Jewish, with Jewish mothers and fathers, is a fact, a historical reality, a shared heredity; nonetheless I believe that religion is incidental to our lives. Being Jewish takes nothing away from the truth of our theories or the scope of our discoveries, nor does it add anything. I'm a mathematician, not a Jewish mathematician. Nor am I a Russian mathematician. I'm the mathematician who solved the Poincaré Conjecture. That's what defines me above all. That's who Grigori Perelman is.

I don't believe in God. I don't believe in the all-powerful God that most Jews address in their sing-song prayers. The idea that there might be a single being that reigns over the Universe with an intelligence superior to my own potential for understanding makes no sense to me. However you look at it, if there were such a God, I would have no means of imagining Him, and I cannot believe in something I cannot imagine. Let's just say it's beyond my abilities. For me, being Jewish is forever limited to the fragile flame that flickered in a corner of the kitchen one night each week at dusk. That doesn't mean I'm not sometimes moved by some form of spirituality, but areas in my life where I come closest to this have nothing to do with religion. The closest thing for me is my intellectual activity. It's what I do to understand how the world works. It's when I'm making common cause with Nature to feel less estranged or foreign to it. The way I commune with the cosmos isn't through prayer or meditation, it's through mathematics. There is no method more radical or powerful for exploring the world.

Many of my friends, my professors and my colleagues at the Steklov Institute believe that to learn about the world you must take trains, planes or boats. They think you need to move to a different city or country and teach at different universities or learn new languages and contemplate unfamiliar landscapes. I see no point. I don't have to go anywhere to expand my understanding. From my office at the Steklov Institute I had a window onto the entire Universe. Some people might see that as a lack of curiosity, but it's really the opposite. Whatever you look at, however far or long you travel the planet, the world you perceive is nothing more than a part of your own self. We carry the essence of the world within us, available and open to anyone ready to make the effort of feeling it. However singular each of us is, we all have the same interior vision. We have the same operating system. There is no sense in looking for truth elsewhere. And the ultimate proof of this homology—of our ability to agree on what is true—is mathematics. Math has no room for debate or argument. What is proven is proven. It's the nec plus ultra *of spirituality and the antithesis of faith.*

Let me tell you another story. I was still a boy—attending that famous Leningrad high school where many of my fellow students were Jews from elsewhere. I used to play at solving the most difficult mysteries in the universe. My favorite pastime was coming up with seemingly insoluble problems and trying to find a key. The enigma of Jesus walking on the water of Lake Tiberias in Galilee was the most difficult of all. It was the puzzle that seemed to me by far the most complex. How could such a miracle occur? How could a man—whom I refused to believe was a god—move across the surface of the water without sinking due to the weight of his body? For several days I made no headway. But then I determined at what speed Jesus would have to be travelling to remain upright on the water, which was actually a fairly simple calculation. Mystery solved. It made no difference to me whether walking at such a speed was humanly possible or not, the enigma itself had vanished. There was no miracle, merely a few mathematical equations and a solution.

John Ball was satisfied. True, one impossible portion of Perelman's soul remained elusive. The one that might contain the tiniest sliver of desire, enough to coax him to the Spanish capital. Nonetheless, the skies had cleared for the chief of the world's mathematicians. His imaginary Grigori had poured his heart out, expressed his most intimate truths and aspirations. In Impressionist strokes, he had indicated to John Ball his inner compass, his cardinal orientations: his love for his mother and for true glory, the deeper meaning of his work, religion and his paradoxical conception of Judaism. There remained only the fourth direction, the least philosophical, the most concrete and profane. The one that tied Perelman to society, and its ultimate symbol, money.

In Russia, money always leads to violence. I used this maneuver to answer a journalist who pressed me about that famous prize of a million dollars the Clay Foundation promised to anyone who proved the Poincaré Conjecture, or any of the six other problems the American philanthropists had pompously baptized "the Millennium Problems." Another story about reporters—you'll probably end up thinking it's a mania. I do admit I'm rather afraid of journalists, even more than of priests. In a confessional at least, the sinner remains out of sight to the inquisitor. Anyway, the Millennium Problems. A thousand years, no less. The human obsession with hogging more than their allotted time is pathetic. The journalist was a typical American female from the East Coast. Blond, prim, teetering on stiletto heels, and compensating for her somewhat strained smile with tortoiseshell reading glasses that betrayed her age. Also, far too convinced of her own intelligence. She had a regular column in some Boston newspaper.

I quickly understood that the only thing that interested her was this famous prize that was to make me a millionaire. A Russian millionaire, no less. No doubt the only one, she suggested, whose fortune was not due to some sordid intrigue involving apparatchiks and fomented in a tower of the Kremlin. She called that her "angle." An obtuse angle, presumably. An angle that barred her from immersing herself in the beauty of abstraction and the mystic reality of concepts. A blind angle also, since it prevented her from understanding that intrigue among mathematicians can be more abject than even the plots of oligarchs.

"You would refuse to accept a million dollars?" she asked me with a touch of irony in her gaze, as though there was only one answer. "Of course I would refuse," I answered. It seemed to me that she was more outraged than incredulous. I had no right to reject such an offer, it would seem. I could tell what she thought: there is no end to his arrogance. What contempt for those who live in poverty. He has no respect for those with limited intellects who will never see such an opportunity. He thinks he's so clever, but his refusal is just childish defiance of our society. But we do the right thing by rewarding achievements with cold hard cash, it's important. What's the point of having such talent if he won't accept fair value?

Of course, what saddened my journalist most was that she would have to change her angle. Forget the heartwarming story of the Russian millionaire! Never mind, she would find an acute angle, pointed and honed with hatred for this crazed mathematician. I became a bearded giant in rags with anachronistic morals, a man awash in an obsolete communist ideology who worked for fame alone. As I watched her twisting around on her chair, her deepest beliefs shaken, tortured by wretched thoughts and probably by an impulse to throttle me, a phrase popped into my mind. "In Russia, money always leads to violence." A crystal-clear affirmation. I enjoy the way it presents as definitive, irrefutable. And it gave me an external reason on which to tether my absurdist choice.

I found my voice—I wasn't refusing this mountain of dough for personal reasons. It wasn't to provoke, or even worse, out of humility, much less out of wisdom. My objection was ethical. It was justified by a responsibility toward Russian society as a whole. How could I possibly accept for mere gain a gift I knew would immediately unleash hatred and violence all around me? What hung in the balance was bigger than me, much bigger.

I had her hooked. I could tell right away. The journalist perched her glasses on top of her head, set her elbows on her knees and stared at me with her mouth agape as though the meaning of the Poincaré Conjecture had come to her in a flash. Her angle had changed again. She'd go for a right angle. Frank, clear and balanced. Her article would tell the story of a modern hero, sacrificing a brilliant future to preserve the peace of Greater Russia. Her mind galloped lightly across the steppes of Central Asia. She saw herself, back in her student days, borrowing a thick volume of Tolstoy from Widener library and nodding off between war and peace with John Harvard looking on.

In Russia, money always leads to violence. It was a statement that had the ring of a self-evident truth. Since the collapse of the

Soviet regime, every glimmer of hope for enrichment set off an explosion of cruelty. Treason, murder, incarceration without trial, sordid attempts at revenge, sometimes years of hard labor in the new Siberian gulags, which were every bit as unpleasant as their Stalinist forebears. The mafia held sway, conducting their affairs in broad daylight. They were proud of their power and sure of their strength. Honest citizens were the ones trying to keep out of sight. When money suddenly erupted in Russia, it was like the entire society had torn off a mask, revealing its true nature. Pandora's box unhinged. Money proved a powerful catalyst for bringing to the surface deep wells of violence that had been buried, choked, institutionalized and contained by the former regime. All of a sudden, they spouted freely, pouring out like lava down the side of a volcano. The totalitarian past mutated, warping into a tidal wave of brutality. The Communist dictatorship had done a thorough job of encouraging a culture of violence among the Russian elite, so much so that they quickly discovered money to be an apt and sophisticated weapon for spreading it.

I was lucky enough—or perhaps unfortunate enough—not to experience this firsthand. I was enjoying the plush surroundings of American universities while the Soviet Union collapsed in chaos. I spent two years at the Courant Institute in New York, then a few semesters in California at UC Berkeley. Not to blow my own horn, but I had built a pretty solid reputation. I had solved several complex topological problems in Riemannian geometry. Elegantly, it was said. Leading universities lined up with offers. Stanford, Princeton, Harvard. No surprise there, I was in their sights. These places feed on the fame of their professors to uphold their reputations. I was offered obscene amounts of money. Nothing like the Clay Foundation's million dollars, but a salary that would have covered the needs of my whole family—what was left of it—for several years. And meanwhile, my friends at the Steklov Institute suffered like hell. They were kicked out of their labs, or else the government stopped paying their salaries—which pretty much came to the same thing in the end: disgrace and poverty. In the new Russia, mathematics was made redundant. As the elites snarled and fought like a pack of dogs over scraps of the former state monopolies, the country's mathematicians starved. I was ashamed of my good luck. To assuage my guilt, I regularly sent money back to Saint Petersburg. At least I could help out needful colleagues. My country was drowning in violence. A society that despises its researchers is a violent society.

Doctors from every possible discipline rushed to the bedside of this ailing society in the early 1990s. Philosophers, politicians, captains of industry, scientists, and, of course, economists. Russia was one big field experiment. A vast, and seemingly virgin territory, an ideal canvas for every Promethean fantasy. The myth of the blank page drew visitors from the West like moths to a candle. The most extreme glimpsed an opportunity for capitalism to exist in its purest incarnation, unsullied by the welfare state. Much the way 19th-century mathematicians deconstructed Euclid's theories to invent a new geometry, economists dreamed of sweeping away the communist past to lay the foundations of a new liberal model. The measures they prescribed for bringing about this true-born capitalism were known as "shock therapy": free pricing and massive privatization of state-owned companies,

*borders thrown open to foreign products. Who knows what else.
I'm no expert. But the term therapy was one I could relate to.*

*Around the same time, I had begun to work on a therapy of my
own. It was a set of surgeries that could be performed on Ricci
flows to complete Hamilton's program. To prove the Conjecture,
Hamilton had developed a strategy. A program, he called it. By
applying a mathematical function known as the Ricci flow, which
is related to heat diffusion, he believed he could transform any
simply connected, closed 3-manifold into a sphere. The Ricci flow
operated like a sort of steam iron. The problem was the program
seemed on the surface to work. But challenging and unexpected
situations quickly cropped up. Singularities, as we call them in
mathematics. Imagine falling into a hole with no bottom, or
confronting infinite crises that there is no way to resolve. The only
way to avoid catastrophe is to anticipate these shocks, identifying
and correcting them with surgeries. As I said, therapy.*

*Since then, I've thought a great deal about parallels between the
Russian economy and topology. Economists worked with an
irregular society as their basic material. It was unequal, lumpy,
swollen here and there with excess certainties, hollow and barren
in other places. Shock therapy involved imposing a radical
program for abolishing all of these imperfections and creating
what economists call an "equal playing field." You have to admit
that this is awfully close to Hamilton's program for correcting the
imperfections of dimension-three spaces. But there was one major
difference. I don't think Hamilton's program could be described as
shock therapy. Our treatment was precise, delicate and subtle. It*

was like the microsurgeries that are performed using microscopes. If I had applied shock therapy to the Ricci flow, I would never have proven the Poincaré Conjecture. Slow, gentle therapy gets results, I've proven it. And I don't see why a cautious approach wouldn't also work in economics.

Unfortunately, economists are short on patience. They don't take the time to examine the implications of their theories. They ignore or deny complexity. But complexity is the key. It is by facing complexity with humility that approaching the truth becomes possible. Right about the time I launched my research into Hamilton's program, economists began experimenting with capitalism in Russia. It took me seven long years to light on the solution to my problem. In that time, seven years, shock therapy had successfully killed off the poor Russian patient.

At any rate, my digressions had taken us far away from the Clay Foundation's million dollars. The Boston reporter seemed more relaxed. A shy smile hovered on her lips and she ran her hands through her hair without thinking. Every so often, she would prompt me to continue with an open question, or just a quizzical nod. I could feel she was more at home with economic models than mathematical concepts. At no point did she take my condemnation personally. The three years she'd spent in the pews of the Harvard Business School, where orthodox economic theory reigned supreme, had not entirely suppressed her capacity for critical thinking. "Money is the instrument of this simplistic vision of the world," I told her. it sounded like a concluding sentence, but I felt the urge to add a personal touch.

I returned to Saint Petersburg in 1995. I turned down all the offers from American universities. I didn't want to teach, it was a waste of time. And easy money would only distract me from my research. In Russia, everything had changed. Everything was for sale. Every sliver of time, every breath of life. My father had flown off to the land he believed was promised him because his ancestors had paid for it with their bodies and their souls. He would have hated what Russia had become. He was enough of a stranger in the old version. The silence and suspicion he had fought against had new causes. Dreams had become sad and tired. The pursuit of liberty had been replaced by the pursuit of money. And in Russia, money always leads to violence.

June 12, 2006

The sun did not rise. Or at least, not to speak of. At best you might say it stretched, like a middle-aged man trying to shake off morning pains. In just two days, John Ball had fallen in tune with these diabolical white nights. At times he had slept without shutting an eye. At others he had remained awake, dreaming deeply all the while. The Northern slumber, in the bright of night. A paradox. Ball was in a hurry. He had barely the time to gulp a cup of hot tea with milk in the hotel's breakfast room, pay his bill and deposit his luggage with the concierge. The latter handed him a ticket with a number for retrieval.

The meeting was set for nine o'clock in front of the main entrance to the Steklov Institute. Mathematicians around the world referred to it as *The Steklov* with that combination of respect and fear inspired by old family estates and haunted castles. Perelman no longer worked there, or had an office. In fact, he hadn't entered once since submitting his resignation in December of the year before. Why had he suggested they meet in front of the Steklov, John wondered. Why had Perelman chosen a place charged with symbolism rather than the anonymity of his hotel's bar or the discreet conference center on the Neva where they had met yesterday? Was it nostalgia for the site of his discoveries on the part of the Russian mathematician? Pure provocation again? Or was it simply the first place that came to mind? Picking up the pace, John Ball considered these various hypotheses and, as usual, refused to choose among them.

It was nine o'clock. The day looked to be hot and muggy, without the slightest protective veil in the sky. John Ball was exhausted from wrestling all night with his angels. He wasn't looking forward to the long walk ahead. A walk that would probably lead nowhere. As he attempted as best he could to gather his thoughts and decide on a strategy, Grigori appeared at the far end of the Fontanka quay. The Russian mathematician strode forward towards his Institute. Suddenly, he halted before the doors. He was wearing the same clothes as before. With his jacket buttoned to the collar, his grim face and hands thrust into the pockets of his pants, he looked about as welcoming as an armored safe. Without offering any kind of greeting or welcome, without even shaking the hand his visitor cautiously extended, Perelman launched into a monologue. It was as though he simply picked up the conversation where he left off the day before.

"I am proud to introduce you to the legendary Steklov Institute, a temple to science and mathematics established by the late Soviet Union. Not what you'd expect, is it? You had hoped for a grander edifice, perhaps. A pediment, some Doric columns, a majestic entrance, no? A commemorative plaque at least, dedicated to the Nobel laureates this institution has produced. Some outward sign of the seething intelligence presumed to be inside. You must be disappointed, John. It's a far cry from the gothic facades, the stained glass and the smooth lawns of Oxford College. Foreigners who come here are generally disappointed. Especially Americans. Their fantasies about Russia tend to threadbare clichés."

As usual, Perelman spoke in an even monotone that betrayed nothing of his mind. Was he being sarcastic or, on the contrary, seeking acknowledgement? Nothing in his expression offered the slightest clue. It was as though he spoke only for himself, and not to be understood at all. You'd think he was standing in front of a microphone, a mirror or a brick wall. Something, at any rate, that was capable of neither sensation nor emotion. To converse with him, you had to take a gamble on decoding the subtext. You had to imagine the real meaning behind the uninflected phrases. John Ball opted for a splash of provocation.

"A temple? Don't tell me you see yourself as a priest, Grigori. I have a hard time imagining you saying mass."

"Perhaps not a temple. But a cloister maybe."

"Either way, temple or cloister, you're an infidel now, if not an actual heretic. You have no seat in the choir. Do you regret leaving the Institute?"

"I haven't left it. I don't climb the steps two by two up to the third floor where my office was, anymore, but my thought is still deeply tied to the Steklov. To its essence. The place itself has lost its purity, unfortunately. Over the last few years, I have felt the outside world creeping in. Insidiously at first, then more blatantly. The walls of the Steklov are porous now. That's the reason why I stepped away. Research demands true isolation. Not to be confused with solitude or the semblance of silence. It must go deeper than that. Anyone who seeks truth must distance himself from the background noise of the world, noise that signifies nothing, contributes nothing. It's all just Brownian motion, preventing you from focusing on the true music of the universe."

"Mathematics, you mean?"

"No. That would be presumptuous. I'm talking about the real music of the universe, the gentle trills of Nature. The truth that precedes and surrounds us. At best, mathematics is simply an effective way for us to connect with this. But anyway, let's go find some coffee. I am going to tell you about Olga."

Naturally, John knew of the celebrated Olga Ladyzhenskaya, although he had never met her. The Steklov must have been a very different place in Olga's day, he mused. She had headed up the mathematical physics department for decades, straight up to her death in 2004. Hers was a legendary research team. Mathematicians all over the world knew well what they owed these pioneers of partial differential equations. And Olga was the soul of the group. She conquered everyone who encountered her. More than her beauty or her extraordinary intellectual force, it was her total devotion to research that did it. That and the attention, affection even, which she lavished on her team. The woman's life had been mangled by the history of her country, and yet she had ungrudgingly contributed her share of fame. Before the war, her father, a math teacher, had been arrested as an enemy of the people and summarily executed. No trial. Until Stalin died, Olga was barred from enrolling at Leningrad University. She was guilty by association, burdened with the legacy of paternal disgrace. The

therapy she chose was to dedicate her life to the discipline her
father had taught.

Perelman, of course, had missed this golden age. When he joined
Olga's department in the mid-nineties, after his dazzling turn in
America, the Steklov was falling apart, literally, due to lack of
repairs. Its professors' salaries were barely above the poverty line.
Most departed, or spent extended periods abroad to teach at foreign
universities. And the standards researchers were held to had
crumbled. Suffering great pains, Olga Ladyzhenskaya had
remained at her post, a stalwart captain going down with the ship.
Perelman, for his part, hardly noticed the deplorable working
conditions. He had returned from the United States with savings
enough to finance his modest lifestyle for several years. A chair
and a desk in a heated room, a computer and a telephone. His needs
were few, just the essentials. He had chosen a life of renunciation,
like a monk. Austere and discreet, authentic and silent, his was an
ascetic existence, a life entirely devoted to mathematics. A therapy
like Olga's, but for a different injury. Or perhaps their wounds were
not so different after all, were they? In Stalin's time, Grigori's
father would likely have suffered the same fate as Olga's.

Ten years after his arrival, Grigori Perelman had resigned from
the Steklov for obscure reasons that prompted wild speculation and
rumor. The letter he sent the Institute's director consisted of a few
laconic sentences, concluding with: "I hereby ask that you accept
my resignation for personal reasons effective January 1st 2006." If
his colleagues' rare disclosures were to be believed, Perelman had
reacted violently to an unsolicited salary increase he had not been

notified of. His friends at the Institute, or those who considered themselves his friends, had thought they were acting in his best interests. A serious misjudgment of Grigori's character. That's exactly what he meant by the infiltration of the outside world. His fame had condemned him to a different status. It shredded the veil of anonymity that protected his peace of mind. The walls of the Steklov no longer protected him from the vast marketplace of ideas where the beauty of a concept was traded for medals or prizes and genius was calculated in net earnings. Perelman could not forgive what he had felt to be an insult. He hadn't turned down a million dollars just to be humiliated over a few hundred rubles.

"You must be disappointed."

The sentence rang for a moment in John Ball's ears. He really hadn't expected anything, but Perelman's assumption artificially planted a feeling of disappointment. The Steklov Institute's main building is a dilapidated five-story edifice with peeling ochre paint. Its location at the far end of Nevsky Prospekt isolates it from the flux of tourists, which is focused on the monuments built along the Neva. The facade runs for some 300 feet along the Fontanka, the left arm of the river, whose current was quelled in the late 18th century by turning it into a canal that encircled the center city. The Fontanka's quays are lined with the former townhouses of Russia's aristocracy. The sidewalks are enhanced with trees, all recently planted. Down below the Steklov, the iron railing made way for a wooden dock. Two blue and white river barges were moored. On deck, employees in uniform were welcoming the day's first customers. A sandwich board announced the prices and duration of various riverboat cruises. A standard tour lasted an hour and brought tourists from the Fontanka to the Moyka before taking the narrow Winter Canal and crossing over to the Neva near the Winter Palace.

The two mathematicians began slowing walking along the canal, breathing in the lazy atmosphere of the summer morning. The quays were practically deserted, exception made for a few scantily clad students. Schoolbags slung over their shoulders, they headed for the last few classes of the year in shorts and t-shirts, seemingly without a care in the world.

John Ball listened to Perelman as the latter told him stories about former times and the Steklov under Olga. Then the conversation veered, taking in their observation of the city and its inhabitants. The environment was less conducive to vast historical recitals than their itinerary of the day before, but Perelman conscientiously pointed out each noteworthy site. Here was a palace that had recently been restored to its former glory, there a street corner where a little-known incident of the October Revolution took place. Further along there were Baroque and Neoclassical buildings that had been home to famous artists: Alexander Pushkin, Ivan Turgenev, Sergei Prokofiev. But despite attempts to summon the souls of these artists to the table, the two men's dialogue was stilted, cold and formal.

It was only some twenty minutes into this grim perambulation that the Russian mathematician finally opened the door of a café. It was a soulless little bar on the ground floor of a cinderblock building from the fifties. The facade was painted black, with yellow Cyrillic letters over the doorway and to the sides that Ball could not make out. A few small tables, all empty, teetered on the sidewalk. Inside, the walls were covered in desilvered mirrors and old black and white photographs in wooden frames. Perelman automatically headed for the back of the room, like a regular customer who assumes his table is reserved for him. He invited Ball to sit. Around them, the bar quickly emptied of its tardy workers and sank into daytime torpor. They ordered the same thing. Espresso, short, with a glass of water.

A murky silence teased and threatened them like the void below a tightrope walker. Nonetheless, John Ball enjoyed such brief suspensions, superficially calm, where the proximity of danger is cloaked by a veil of ignorance. He considered a last attempt at convincing Perelman. As a symbolic gesture. Since the mysterious revelations of the night before, he knew, of course, that the matter was closed. The oracle had spoken. Grigori would not go to Madrid. And it would be John's thankless task to report this news to a roomful of outsize egos, all feigning surprise. His job to fend off the hordes of reporters all curious and hungry for scandal. His responsibility to handle the disappointment of the Spanish authorities, and probably also to foil greedy attempts by those Chinese researchers to secure the prize, right down to the wire. Fine. He would fulfil his appointed task. Perform his duty. Do everything possible to protect what was most important—the reputation of the mathematical community.

Surprisingly, it was Perelman himself who brought the topic back around to the Englishman's business. As though he'd read the other's mind.

"Hold on, John. Let's be serious for a minute. Do you know what that Arthur Jaffe character who is president of the Clay institute told one of my friends, a great Russian mathematician who asked him why he'd offered a million-dollar prize?"

"No, not the foggiest."

He said: "You have no idea how Americans live. When politicians, businessmen and housewives see that you can earn a million dollars doing math, they'll stop discouraging their children from becoming mathematicians and pressuring them to become doctors, lawyers or other high-earning professionals."

"Very interesting," answered Ball with a smile. "So you see, that million dollars was for a good cause after all! Isn't that what you call encouraging well-heeled girls and boys to enter a profession as tedious and poorly compensated as mathematicians?"

"My mother wanted me to be a great mathematician. She said it was a noble calling."

"Your mother is not American, Grigori. She's a Russian intellectual. The only political system she ever really knew was an unyielding and brutal collectivism. And, if I may say so, she is most of all a Jewish mother, proud and stubborn."

"You're quite right. I had no idea you knew my mother so well," answered Perelman, agreeing to the exchange of smiles. "I am less and less fond of the way my own compatriots live, but it's likely that I will never understand the American lifestyle."

"You're not the only one! For an Englishman who comes from a long line of Midlands gentry, the liberal tendencies of Americans are peculiar. Almost as bizarre as they must seem to a Communist Russian."

The symbolic gesture petered out. Ball had laid down his arms like a gentleman. It was a right and proper surrender. Perelman paid their bill, dropping a few coins on the table. Cheerfully, the two intellectuals got up to leave the dingy bar. Moments later, they emerged, blinded by the sunlight, at the intersection of two wide and undistinguished avenues. The sun hung almost overhead, reverberating off the pale facades of the buildings. They had left the beating heart of the city behind and found themselves catapulted to an earlier era. Here, the sad Soviet years had so saturated every stone that no repointing could ever erase them entirely.

John Ball wished he could read his companion's mind. He wanted to get back inside Perelman's subconscious, shouldering aside taboo to seize pieces of forbidden truth. He tried to marshal his thoughts and make his way back to the trance he had fallen into the night before, but it was no good. The harder he concentrated, the more his own suffering echoed in his head, repeating on a loop, over and over. Most of the time he had no fear of silence, assuming it didn't last too long and hit that undefinable limit beyond which the lack of speech between two men becomes physically uncomfortable. Past that point lies the realm of the dead. Silence reigns and human beings are mere ghosts. Filled with panic, they struggle, attempting to flee their mute bondage. Too late, the darkness drinks up their voices.

They pushed on. Perelman had resumed his ferocious pace, as though he determined to end it all. He strode along, deciding, directing. "He's got the home advantage," thought John Ball, thinking wistfully of the World Cup matches he could be peacefully watching on TV if he hadn't accepted this idiotic ambassadorship. He began to fear the fatal blow, the moment their silence would become irreversible. If that happened, he mustn't blame Perelman, he told himself. He himself was just as guilty. After all, it takes two to engage in conversation, it must take two to achieve total silence.

Ball could have found solace in the stereotypes that biographies of the eccentric Russian were littered with, but he considered that beneath him. Perelman was generally described as being autistic, dysfunctional, an asocial hermit type. Sometimes he was painted as a sort of monster, caged in by his communicative limitations. But it was not so. The man Ball had encountered was sensitive, open and cultivated. He was an accessible and affable human being, once the wary business of mutual observation dispatched. He had expected anxious stuttering and difficulties forming words or phrases. What he'd experienced was mostly a fluid exchange, leaping from architecture to philosophy, from Renaissance art to deep musings on contemporary society. Perelman had turned out to be an accomplished musician, a fan of opera, and above all, an inexhaustible fount of knowledge when it came to the history of his country. Ball had been worried he would find himself faced with a mulish, arrogant mathematician, a closed-minded misanthrope who lived disconnected from reality, blinded by his own brilliance. Miraculously, he had enjoyed the man's company, and indeed felt empathy for Perelman.

While punctuated with much arm-wrestling and a few sparks, their exchanges seemed to the Englishman to have revealed the secret code by which an exceptional man lived. He felt he knew where Perelman's fears lay, understood the suffering his pathological modesty caused him, his complex psychoanalytic inheritance—all the many branching ramifications that vulgar observers, from jealous mathematicians to celebrity reporters seeking a Dostoyevskian hero had purposefully exaggerated into a caricature.

Autism is an open mystery—*terra incognita*. It's an unexplored continent, a wilderness that frightens people, like a glacial desert, frozen and still. We assume that inside all is unutterable sadness, a depression so deep and wide that the victim bars the door from the inside. Or else we imagine some intellectual deficiency. Or dementia.

The autism Perelman lived with, at any rate, was nothing like that. Grigori was neither crazy nor stupid. He had nothing in common with Hesse's Steppenwolf, nothing of the stubborn ascetic withdrawing from the world out of melancholy or in order to achieve Buddhist serenity. "A man cannot live intensely except at the cost of the self," wrote Hermann Hesse. Perelman had renounced intensity, and self-harm was not on his agenda. John Ball had discovered a being who was regretfully asocial, but not tortured, unrepentant. A man at peace whose humility was ontological. He was a man who didn't think about his absence from the world, because that was simply how he lived.

Faced with this man, whose gaze still reflected the fury and innocence of childhood, Ball could not rally extenuating circumstances. Autism and insanity were not the issue. If this silence were to take root, it would be his fault, and he would carry the burden clear to Madrid. A sudden idea came to him. It was only a twinkle, not much to go on, but still, a light at the end of the tunnel. He decided to ask a question that was subtler than it seemed. A question that straddled the everyday, the way you might straddle a parapet to jump into the void.

"By the way, I almost forgot to wish you a happy birthday, Grigori. It's tomorrow, no? Are you planning any kind of celebration? A gathering among friends?

"Thank you. It is indeed tomorrow. I will be forty."

"The age limit for the Fields Medal!"

"Yes indeed, my expiration date! If I'd been born just a year earlier, you might have been saved this painful trip, John. Things are so contingent. The grand jury of mathematical minds would have sensibly put me in the discard pile. I would have been consigned directly to the elephant graveyard of academia, with every other researcher who failed to prove something really useful before losing half their neurons."

"But look at it the other way. What if the coincidence were a sign? A matter of fate? The clock striking at exactly the right hour?"

"Then it would simply illustrate how badly destiny can miss the mark sometimes. And it would show why it is synonymous with injustice. Is it destiny that precludes me from sharing this honor with Richard Hamilton? Hamilton will be sixty-three soon. He submitted his dissertation the year I was born. Just think about it. Much too ancient, old professor Hamilton. Not worthy to receive a pretty medal from the hands of the King of Spain. Good thing William Thurston got lucky faster. What would I ever have succeeded in proving if Thurston and Hamilton hadn't come before me?"

"We all move forward in the footsteps of those who precede us. That's what history is. Mountain climbers know all about this unfair distribution. For an ascent, it's the Sherpas who carry the baggage and assemble the tents. But they remain at base camp, looking up while a few climbers make it to the top. Posterity doesn't record the name of those who bore the burden. It's a shame, but that's how it is. Richard Hamilton was your Sherpa, in a manner of speaking."

"Absolutely not. I won't let you even think such nonsense. According to you, the absolutely brilliant application of the Ricci Flow, the idea that by letting it work, one might unify the curvature of variations at which it is not constant, the genius intuition that the flow would sometimes come to a standstill because a variant's curvature would explode, the idea that these singularities must be understood and classified, the patient, surgical removal of areas that collapse to start the flow back up on another piece, the hope that after some finite number of surgeries one might obtain a constantly curved piece. All those epiphanies and insights, nothing but groundwork, you say? Logistics? You're wrong John. Wrong. What Richard Hamilton did was not setting up tents or carrying baggage. Posterity will remember Perelman as the methodical and prudent climber who ascended the peak that was Hamilton."

"If you say so. Such modesty becomes you, but the gratitude you owe your predecessors will not change the verdict of posterity one bit. History is like a magnet. One polarity attracts, the other repels. You are at the positive end. Resistance is futile. And frankly, I will say that in my view, History's magnet made the right choice this time. Richard Hamilton is doubtless a great mathematician. But at this point, he is no longer able to distinguish between genius and plagiarism. He congratulated some random Chinese postdocs who have shamefully cribbed your work and pretend to find imaginary flaws in your reasoning. Meanwhile, he didn't bother to congratulate you after the enlightening presentation of your work you gave at Columbia."

"You were at Columbia?"

"I certainly was. I wouldn't have missed it for the world. Every mathematician who could get in was in a tither. Most of them were hoping against hope for the culminating moment when you would throw your arms up to heaven and announce: 'Tis done. I have proven the Poincaré Conjecture!' What they got was an hour of explanation on the properties of certain partial derivative equations.

All right, most were probably not equipped to understand what you were saying. But Richard Hamilton? Why the silence? I was watching you as you gave your concluding remarks. I could see the disappointment in your eyes. You stepped off the stage and walked to the front row where he was sitting to shake his hand. A swarm of students and academics hovered to watch the exchange between master and disciple, waiting to catch the smile, the passing of the baton, an anointment. But nothing happened. No comments, no questions. Richard Hamilton stalked off without a word, as though he'd just attended a rather disappointing dissertation defense. That day, Hamilton condemned himself to the basecamp forever."

"Disappointment is the flip side of hope and expectation. It is generally a good idea not to have high expectations when it comes to human beings."

"So, are you celebrating your birthday?" Ball countered, doubling back on his subject, like a lawyer, pleased with his cross-examination, who seeks to close the debate while ahead.

"Until I turned thirteen, Mama used to bake me a traditional apple cake. She would serve it with a candle on top. Always just one candle. Maybe that explains why I'm not very sensitive to the passing of time. I haven't celebrated it for a long time now. But if you stay one more day in Saint Petersburg, you can come have dinner with us at home.

"I am very touched, Grigori. It would have been a great pleasure to meet your mother, but I am expected back in England. I too have family obligations. My plane leaves tonight at six o'clock. And besides, I know for certain now, that you would refuse the only gift I'm in a position to offer you."

"I'll walk you back to your hotel," said Perelman with a forced smile.

The two mathematicians turned back towards the river. They walked more slowly now. Their footsteps were heavy, as though a blanket of melancholy were cast over them, the heavy weight of despondency. One after another they crossed the various canals, picking their way through the Venice of the North. First the Fontanka, its quays lined with colorful palaces and the Lomonosov Bridge, with its squat, domed towers and moveable midsection. Then came the narrower Griboyedov Canal, with its more private feel. At last they reached the Moyka, its banks studded with skiffs and barges, its bridges with their colorful and evocative names like Green Bridge, Lantern Bridge and the romantic Bridge of Kisses. The Kempinski Hotel was nearby, but it was too early to part company. Perelman suggested they walk to the Neva. John Ball soon recognized the streets ran through to the back of the Hermitage, followed by the Alexander Garden. The surroundings were cheerful and variegated. The tourists added a diversity that gave Saint Petersburg the air of a cosmopolitan city. At every street corner there were stalls piled high with Russian nesting dolls and chess sets—all hand painted, according to the merchants hawking their wares. There was also every sort of Red Army surplus item.

A change had come over the two men and the atmosphere between them as well. They had the look of two travelers headed for home. Two fishermen steering for the harbor, limbs stiff and eyes reddened from fighting against the elements. Whatever the catch, the sight of a solid shore is welcome. Between them, all hostilities had ended. Full truce. A sense of levity floated on the air. Perelman recounted childhood memories. John Ball cracked jokes, skewering some of their mutual acquaintances and laughing at the narrow-mindedness of his colleagues at the International Mathematical Union.

"Just imagine the confusion and panic on their faces when I give them a summary of my trip. I will speak frankly, I promise. I'll tell them... This is what I'll tell them. "I went to Saint Petersburg and I conversed extensively with Grigori Perelman. He is in full possession of his faculties, fully decided, and he has convinced me that his decision was the right one. Not only is he justified in not coming to Madrid, but the most sensible course of action for us would be to cancel the Congress and immediately dissolve our reactionary and anachronistic body. Math is being stifled, mathematics requires fresh air, and today, that air blows on the Baltic Sea." At this, Perelman let out a shout of laughter that sounded like it belonged to someone else.

It was barely noon when John Ball and Grigori Perelman reached the portico of the Kempinski hotel. The doorman greeted the Englishman warmly, probably remembering the considerable tip of the day before. The two men walked into the lobby, which struck them as dark after the midday sun. Ball had another four hours before the town car he'd ordered that very morning would roll up to take him to the Poulkovo airport. He would leave the city without bitterness and with a sense of duty accomplished. He had come, he had seen, and he had been forced to admit defeat.

The two preceding days had shaken him profoundly. He had met a singular individual, a hybrid being with the morals of a spoiled child perched in the body of a giant off the steppes. There is no coming away from such an encounter unscathed. They turned to face each other, eye to eye. Perelman thanked the Englishman for coming and held Ball's hand in his own for a long moment. Then, as the Russian was turning to leave and re-enter the ascetic life he had stepped out of for a moment, John Ball lifted his index finger and beckoned to his host, as though he'd forgotten some crucial detail. Like that famous American TV detective in the beige raincoat used to do near the end of each episode.

"I have one last question for you, Grigori, if you don't mind."

"Of course not. Please go ahead."

"Suppose your father were to attend the Fields Medal awards ceremony in Madrid. Would that change your mind?"

"That's absurd. You know it as well as I do. Your question rests on a faulty hypothesis. It is strictly rhetorical. My father belongs to an entirely different space-time. Your suggestion is no more plausible than if you were to promise me that Moses, or Jesus, or God himself would attend. I cannot answer, whatever I said would be meaningless."

"Fine. Let us say that what I'm suggesting is a variation on *reductio ad absurdum.* Don't tell me you've never purposefully set out deliberately on a dead-end path merely to lift the veil of the impossible for a second and use those insights to attack reality with renewed force?"

"Naturally. But this is not about mathematics."

"So? There are holes to be repaired in every area, in every nook and cranny of our lives. You taught me that."

"You are most formidable, my friend."

"Well then? Would it change your mind?"

"My father lives on another planet. He inhabits a closed and secret world, a universe so dense and luminous that you and I have no power to understand it. It is the opposite of a black hole, a place where truth is like the air itself, so present, so ubiquitous, there is no need for math. My father is seventy-two years old. He left Russia twenty years ago. I have only seen him twice since then. Today, he never leaves his little apartment except to pray or to study at one of his Orthodox neighborhood's synagogues in Jerusalem. Come to think of it, you're right, a *reductio ad absurdem* is not so absurd after all.

I will answer your question, since it is the last one, and because you have shown me there is no escaping it. If the fabric of time were torn somehow... If the impossible somehow became reality... If the worlds that seem so incompatible today were to touch at some shared tangent... If our parallel fates were to somehow cross before infinity, as in non-Euclidian space, then, yes. In that case, I might indeed find myself wearing a dark suit and a white shirt, choking behind a too-tight bow tie, standing shakily on a stage in front of a monarch in full regalia, reaching out my hand. And to me, the prize

I received would represent all the meaning and intelligence in the universe. Just because there would be a little old man in a black kippah sitting in the front row, thin and bald. A man moved to tears with joy and pride, just like when I used to solve the logic problems he set me when I was eight."

"Thank you, Grigori. I didn't come for nothing."

September 1, 2006

The International Congress of Mathematicians opened in Madrid on August 22, 2006, just a few dozen miles from Spain's former capital, Toledo. There, nine centuries earlier, Gerard of Cremona had been the first to make Latin translations of the great Arabic treatises on mathematics. His work had served to launch a frenzy of extraordinary intellectual activity in Europe. The event was very grand and conducted to perfection by the distinguished Sir John Ball. He proved an excellent master of ceremonies, sparing none of his phlegmatic charm and deft diplomacy.

As expected, Grigori Perelman's absence and his refusal to accept the Fields Medal were on everyone's lips. Never had a gathering of mathematicians attracted so many reporters from international press pools, TV stations and radio broadcasts. The real drama, however, had unfolded backstage over the prior months, far from the crowd and sealed from rumor, in silence. The publication by Cao and Zhu did not withstand close scrutiny by experts. The sin of haste had gotten the better of the two postdocs. Entire passages of their paper copied the work of mathematicians Bruce Kleiner and John Lott. Worse yet, they had neglected to acknowledge their sources. The great wall of China was full of cracks.

In his inaugural address, John Ball delivered a scathing indictment: "While celebrating this feast of mathematics, with the many talking points that it will provide, it is worth reflecting on the ways in which our community functions. Mathematics is a profession of high standards and integrity. We freely discuss our work with others, without fear of it being stolen, and research is communicated openly prior to formal publication. Editorial procedures are fair and proper, and work gains its reputation through merit and not by how it is promoted. These are the norms operated by the vast majority of mathematicians. The exceptions are rare, and they are noticed..."

On the third day of the Congress, John Morgan began his lecture with a sentence that left no room for doubt: "Grigori Perelman has proven the Poincaré Conjecture." Shortly later, Richard Hamilton pronounced himself "very grateful to Grisha for finishing it." Cornered, Cao and Zhu made a last ditch change to the title of their article, presenting it as an exegesis of Perelman's proof. Game over.

The Congress had ended the week before, and John Ball was back in London. He rather appreciated the cool weather after the blazing heat of Madrid. He knew he would look back on the period that had just drawn to a close as the most exciting and exhausting of his entire life. At the moment, though, his only desire was to enjoy a few weeks of rest at home with his family in Oxford, where he could spend his days reading and ambling around the countryside, punctuated with high tea at the appointed time. He knew, however, that his work was far from finished. There was the after-sales service to deliver. He would have to hone and polish the narrative of this historic moment for it to stand the test of time.

This is what prompted him to yield to the proddings of journalists, while insisting on vetting the select list himself. Among them were emmissaries from the British dailies, a few leading specialists from learned periodicals, and a few French reporters with a passion for Poincaré. There were also London correspondants of Russian media such as *Moskovski Komsomolets* and *Komsomolskaïa Pravda*. Over in Red Square, the myth of Russia's new hero was taking shape. Paper statues were erected to Grigori Perelman. He was described as a brilliant, tortured mind, egocentric and borderline crazy, but also as a simple soul, humble and pure. A free spirit, profoundly human. He was a true patriot, deeply attached to both the motherland and his mother. He was called an atypical science type, a solitary man who drew inspiration from contemplation, and at the same time an excessive figure, larger than life, aggressive and uncompromising. An unstable individual whose behavior was sometimes absurd. And a man who ultimately shut himself in and autodestructed. How could such a character, who seemed to step out of a novel, fail to win over those busy penning the story of a New Russia? Did he not have something of the Dostoyevskian hero?

John Ball read through his remarks several times. He fielded questions from reporters, but stuck closely to his notes. He had no intention of improvising. He knew himself well enough to know he was not comfortable with this exercise. He worried about slipping off message or saying too much. Worse, he was afraid any silence or hesitation on his part would be freely interpreted by journists. In Madrid, he had found the right words. He had affirmed cardinal principles and calmed the turmoil that had taken hold of the mathematical microcosm. His main concern now was to defend the honor of his profession before the public at large. All the ingredients to kindle unhealthy curiosity in the press were assembled, and could easily lead to a giant smear campaign. Picture it. On the one hand we have a genius, a man of inegrity defying his peers. On the other, we see a bunch of cutthroat researchers, stooping to anything to claim a million-dollar prize. And all this unfurls, if you please, in an explosive geopolitical environment where China and Russia vie for world domination as America's philanthropists look on, baffled. The media must not be allowed to contrast the integrity of a single man with the cynicism of an entire system. That would be a catastrophe.

Picking his way through this difficult situation, John Ball knew that his strongest suit was the figure of Grigori Perelman himeself. He saw the advantage to be gained by drawing on the sympathy the Russian mathematician inspired. His strategy was a simple one. He would emphasize his closeness to Grisha, as he called him. "I have great news for you," he started. "We all owe a debt of gratitude to Grisha. Today, you may finally sleep more soundly: the only simply connected three-manifold around which any loop of string can be contracted to a point is a dimension-three sphere." The correspondants from scientific publications grinned. Mainstream journalists cast sidelong glances their way for a cue and followed suit, pretending to understand. That broke the ice. Ball could move on to more serious matters. He talked about his trip to Saint

Petersburg and his long talks with Perelman. He confessed that he had come away from the experience with a conviction: in no way was Perelman's refusal of the Fields Medal a way of throwing down the gauntlet. It was neither "defiance" nor "contempt." Attributing such motives to Perelman was insulting, he continued. This decision could only be explained by the Russian's "feeling of isolation from the scientific community," to the extent that "he did not wish to represent it or become its figurehead." Questions began buzzing around the room. Ball listened, consulted his notes, and answered, sticking to his story. "He was offered the prize and, despite himself, has become a figurehead and an object of awe and scandal."

The strategy paid off. Show over. The masters of algebra and geometry would be free to resume their stately pace and retreat to the discretion of their parallel universe. But one heavenly body had definitively departed from the dance. Instead, a new star would shine brightly among the constelations of popular mythology.

Paris, June 9, 2010

Epilogue

It was just before eight o'clock on the morning of Wednesday, the 9th of June, 2010. The taxi John Ball had hired to take him to the Gare du Nord rolled past the entrance to the Sainte-Chapelle and along the length of the Conciergerie on the Île de la Cité to cross the Seine River over the Pont-au-Change bridge. Changing his habits for once, the former head of the International Mathematical Union had stayed at a charming little hotel on the Left Bank, nestled between the Luxembourg gardens and the Place Saint Sulpice. From there, it had been only a short walk across the park and up the hill via the Rue Soufflot to the Institut Henri Poincaré.

Violent thunderstorms had torn through the capital all night, electrifying the lightening rods on top of the city's monuments and TV antennas on the roofs of buildings. When Paris awoke, evidence of the storm could be seen on the pavement. Puddles oozed between crooked paving stones and odd objects were randomly littered about. Above the slate rooftops, the white sky unfolded like a soul newly released from purgatory, its sins all washed away. John Ball looked east through the window of his cab. The sun resembled a huge ceramic ball tinged with orange. Its surface looked imperfect, pocked and grainy, like a sculpture made by human hands. A real work of art, he told himself, not like those smooth and shiny things by Jeff Koontz. Little by little, in the pale light, the star we call our own emerged from its apparent slumber. It was still possible for a moment or two, to look at it directly without being blinded. John Ball thought back to the prior day. Once again, he had had to put up with lectures by various academic pontiffs praising Grigori Perelman for his fantastic proof of the Poincaré Conjecture. Once again, the most learned speeches and those of the ignorant were similarly brimming with superlatives. Once again, as in Madrid four years earlier, the lecture hall was packed, the audience still and attentive. And, once again, Grigori Perelman had been absent.

At 11 o'clock on Tuesday the 9th of June, John Ball had made his way to the top of the Montagne Saint-Geneviève. Number 11 Rue Pierre et Marie Curie, to be precise. Here on this particular hill, students from the Sorbonne, the École Normale Supérieure and the École Polytéchnique are thrown together. The air crackles, saturated with centuries of intelligence. Ball sat down in the front-row seat reserved for him at the main lecture hall of the Institut Henri Poincaré. Next to him sat several French recipients of the Fields Medal. Mathematicians from all over the world crowded into the room, jostling to attend this historic event. It was an exceptional occasion. They had gathered in this building dedicated to Poincaré to celebrate the resolution of one of the most enduring and fascinating puzzles in the history of mathematics. Certainly, more than a few of those in the room had dreamed of being the one to conquer it.

The ceremony began. The Institute's director got up and delivered a few words of welcome, seemingly off the cuff. He spoke hurriedly, as though rushing through the task as quickly as possible. In all likelihood he was trying to leave as much time as possible for Valérie Pécresse, the French government's Minister for Higher Education and Research. Soon, she strode onto the stage, the worn wooden stairs creaking under her heeled shoes. She was an elegant young woman with a broad smile, mid-thirties or thereabouts. Her severe black suit was closed over a white blouse buttoned all the way up. She wore her wavy blond hair shoulder length. Impeccably styled. She deposited her notes on the lectern. Nothing in her attitude suggested she was the least bit intimidated by the assembly of mathematicians before her. The powerful are all alike in being difficult to impress. Or perhaps it is precisely because they aren't easily impressed that they come to be the men and women of power they are? John Ball smiled, imagining the scene in reverse. How would Grigori Perelman look speaking to a hall filled with heads of state and ministers. Why did the mere idea seem so absurd?

The minister cast a searching look around the room. She fixed her smile, adjusted the lectern's microphone and waited for silence. You need to hear a heartbeat, her mentor had once told her. Could she really fathom the importance of the moment? After all, this speech, which had been in her calendar for ages, was just one item in her day, a time slot like any other in her planner. She might be addressing business school students or future art historians in a couple of hours. She could be having lunch with a team of scientists from China or South Africa. Such is the daily grind of a politician.

She had long forgotten her life as a specialist of Internet and Communications law. Her standing as a government minister gave her leave to talk about just about anything, including complex notions of geometry and topology. And she fully availed herself of the privilege.

As fate would have it, the conference was held in a rather tense political context. For several weeks, academics from the French public institutions had been locked in a struggle with their minister. They were firmly opposed to the creation of a performance bonus system. Should researchers' compensation really be tied to the number of publications they managed to place in international peer reviewed journals? This question had raised a tempest in the teacup of France's research community.

Academics demanded total freedom in choosing the topics they would pursue. They worried that these bonuses would siphon the best minds away from the difficult questions, complex problems that might take years of work. For her part, the minister emphasized the importance of added value and the need to be competitive internationally. Total deadlock. Obviously, the debate brought to mind the famous Clay Foundation's million-dollar prize. Was it right to promise a million dollars to the person who succeeded in solving the Poincaré Conjecture? Was Perelman unwittingly siding with academics against the minister? That very morning, an op-ed wondered whether "the rot of finance and commerce" had not taken root in the realm of mathematics, a world believed to be pure and clean.

The minister began her speech with expressions of gratitude tailored to the circumstances. She thanked the officials present, the Institut Poincaré and its directors, the Clay Foundation, which had jointly organized the event, and even the genius of French mathematicians, renewed with each passing generation. Her introduction was too long and hyperbolic. Finally, she got to the meat of the matter. In her mind, she focused on her two objectives. Pay a stirring tribute to Grigori Perelman. Yield no ground to opponents of her reform of academic compensation. She began by recalling that when he formulated his conjecture, the illustrious Henri Poincaré had scribbled a premonitory phrase at the bottom of the page: "but this question would take us too far afield." "It is one thing," she said, "to believe you recognize a truth. It is an entirely different thing to prove it," she concluded. Then she became more animated. "There you have, ladies and gentlemen, a marvelous definition of mathematics: the study of questions that take us too far afield."

Sitting in his front row seat, Sir John Ball choked. Several thousand miles away, in his modest retreat in a suburb of Saint Petersburg, Grigori Perelman must have felt a sudden pain steal through his entire body. So this young minister had understood the whole thing? She launched without hesitation into a critical analysis of the abnormal. Grigori Perelman, a genius among geniuses, had become an alien. He was the archetype of those mathematician types who take us too far afield, leading us astray in a realm of concepts and abstraction that is not our own. "His very absence today is a sign. It affirms the meaning of an existence devoted to mathematics, driven by a passion to study mathematics for its own sake." The mystery was no more. Absence provided the irrefutable proof. Grigori Perelman no longer belonged to our world. A million dollars had not sufficed to draw him back into the society of normal human beings. Peace be with him.

The taxi stopped for a moment at a traffic light before pushing its way laboriously onto the Place du Chatelet. The heavy morning traffic allowed John Ball to stare, a trifle defiantly, at the enormous orange ball rising over the Théâtre de la Ville, the buildings on the Quai de Gesvres and further on, the Hôtel de Ville de Paris. It was precisely at this moment that the famous question posed by Leibniz popped into his mind. "Why is there something, rather than nothing?" He thought again about the horrid ceremony he'd attended the day before and its false tribute. A farce. He kicked himself for having agreed to participate in such a charade. Leibniz was wrong, he told himself. That's not the right question. Too abstract, too disembodied, too philosophical. The question needling him at that moment was more personal, more physical. An egotistical, human question: "Why is there something I don't understand?" Is that not the ultimate question for any researcher? The spectacle of the world this morning seemed to him so true, so obvious, so simple. The ball of fire, so reminiscent of a giant toy, rose into the sky like a helium balloon. It was positively bursting with truth, it literally filled your eyes. How can this thing exist when I can't manage to understand it?

John Ball cast his mind back to the long walk along the Neva with Grigori. It had been four years ago at the beginning of this very month, June. Four years already. He found this whiff of the past an agreeable sensation. A gentle nostalgia. He could remember the interminable silences, the awkwardness that had set in between himself and the Russian mathematician. He recalled his hopes and his anger. He recalled the fissures he had ventured into. One particular exchange came back to him, about Grothendieck, that other hermit mathematician, the other recalcitrant genius. Perhaps the answer lies there, he thought. Grothendieck had written in one of his treatises, "The simple appears complicated, complexity appears simple." Complexity appears simple. The warm sunshine is self-evident, mused the Englishman. Its color and shape are familiar. It appears to me simple, true, undeniable, and yet I cannot explain that it is here, instead of nothing. In order to pierce this mystery, I would have to be willing to give up the obvious. I would need to lift the veil, throw caution to the wind and plunge into the frightening infinity of complexity. Had Grigori Perelman found the key, he asked himself? Had he found the confidence necessary to dive into the unknown, like Icarus defying the laws of physics? The crucial thing about the proof of the Poincaré Conjecture, its essence then, was not the answer, as everyone thought. It was the method.

Ball had returned to London.

After the Congress in Madrid, a friend of his—a non-mathematician as his academic friends used to say jokingly—had landed a sharp quip with an acid tongue. "Fabulous conjecture there, John. A sphere is a sphere. Corking, really!" It was only a jealous stab by a philistine, but it touched him more deeply than its author could have guessed. If Perelman had achieved his state of nirvana, it was because he had refused to bow to simplicity. He had ventured into forbidden territory and explored places that had terrified everyone before him. It was because his intuition led him to the frontier of the unknowable.

Grigori Perelman's genius lay in understanding that the simpler reality is, the more complex the path to truth.

Author's Note

The meeting between Grigori Perelman and John Ball in Saint Petersburg during June of 2006 is matter of record. Sir John Ball flew to the shores of the Baltic Sea in order to convince Perelman to attend the Congress in Madrid and receive the Fields Medal. On the evening of his arrival, he did indeed watch Britain's first 2006 World Cup soccer match at a sports bar in the city. It is also true that Perelman and Ball did a great deal of walking over the course of their two days together. There is also no doubt that Perelman immediately dismissed the English mathematician's proposal.

That about covers the sum of factual material.

These details were generously provided by Sir John Ball himself. What happened was this. As I was preparing to write this novel in 2014, I decided to get in touch with Professor Ball directly. I had noted that his official biography included a role on an Expert Committee at a major French corporation and concluded that he must speak French. Nonetheless, I wrote to him in English, suggesting via email that we meet when and wherever would be most convenient for him. A few hours later, my inbox contained his reply: "I'll be in Paris briefly next week. Let's have dinner." Which is what we did.

We met the following Monday evening in the lobby of his hotel next to the Arch de Triumph. From there we went to the nearest bistro. After ordering a meal and wine, we chatted for some two hours. Ball spoke excellent French. He seemed delighted to talk about the episode, although it was impossible for me to tell whether he remembered the experience as pleasant or unpleasant. He said he found my idea of writing about Perelman interesting and shared several anecdotes from behind the scenes at the Congress. He also explained the imbroglio surrounding the Chinese mathematicians' publication, and filled me in on his exchanges with reporters. But he proved evasive whenever my questions focused on Grigori Perelman himself, his underlying motives, his supposed autism. He would say nothing about the Russian's relationship with his mother or especially with his father. "Some things are confidential," he told me. "What he and I said to each other is between us."

Most of the biographical details about Perelman are corroborated, having been borrowed from various sources[2]. Here, I am thinking especially of references to his childhood, his studies, his enthusiasm for chess, his time in the United States and publication of his research. These can be found in the few published materials concerning the mathematician.

I have purposefully kept descriptions of Perelman's work itself to a minimum, sticking strictly to basics. My knowledge of mathematics is too sketchy and too far back. Should anyone wonder, my description of the Poincaré Conjecture from the first chapter was inspired by a French website, ABC Maths (http://abcmaths.free.fr/gregory perelman.htm).

---

[2] Masha Gessen, *Perfect Rigor*, Houghton Mifflin Harcourt, 2009 and Sylvia Nasar and David Gruber, *Manifold Destiny*, New Yorker, August 21, 2006.

The exchanges between the two mathematicians are invented. Some may draw on things either Perelman or Ball is known or imputed to have said at some point. There being no witnesses to report what happened during those two days, I have taken the liberty of reimagining them. Obviously, I have never met Grigori Perelman. He has had no contact with the outside world since 2006. What you have just read is a work of fiction, a novel. While the main characters may be inspired by Grigori Perelman and John Ball, the words I have attributed to them mostly express my own concerns and questions.